SNOWFLAKE KISSES

"Save me!" cried a laughing Mary Ann, running around a tree with her nephews and their dog in pursuit.

She ran right into Lionel's arms, and he held her close for a moment as they were pelted with snowballs at knee level and the boys screamed with glee at Mary Ann's spirited cries of dismay.

"Are you cold?" he asked, looking down into Mary Ann's laughing eyes when the boys and the dog ran off. She was trembling in her snow-encrusted burgundy pelisse.

Her smile faded.

"Not anymore," she said gravely as she snuggled more closely into his arms.

He curled one finger around a damp ringlet. Her hair was hanging in soggy strings, her nose was red, and never had she looked so beautiful to him. She was irresistible. He bent to taste her pretty, cherry-red lips, but Mary Ann laid a hand against his chest to prevent him.

"Lionel," Mary Ann whispered with regret in her eyes. "We are in plain sight of the parlor window."

"So we are," he replied huskily as he drew her into the cover of a nearby clump of trees and bushes. . . .

Books by Kate Huntington

THE CAPTAIN'S COURTSHIP

THE LIEUTENANT'S LADY

LADY DIANA'S DARLINGS

MISTLETOE MAYHEM

A ROGUE FOR CHRISTMAS

Published by Zebra Books

A ROGUE
FOR
CHRISTMAS

Kate Huntington

ZEBRA BOOKS
Kensington Publishing Corp.
http://www.zebrabooks.com

ZEBRA BOOKS are published by

Kensington Publishing Corp.
850 Third Avenue
New York, NY 10022

All Kensington titles, imprints, and distributed lines are available at special quantity discounts for bulk purchases for sales promotion, premiums, fund-raising, educational or institutional use.

Special book excerpts or customized printings can also be created to fit specific needs. For details, write or phone the office of the Kensington Special Sales Manager: Kensington Publishing Corp., 850 Third Avenue, New York, NY 10022. Attn. Special Sales Department Phone: 1-800-221-2647.

Zebra and the Z logo Reg. U.S. Pat. & TM Off.

First Printing: October 2001
10 9 8 7 6 5 4 3 2 1

Printed in the United States of America

*This book is dedicated to my husband,
Robert Chwedyk, and to his parents,
Wanda and Thaddeus Chwedyk,
with much love and appreciation.*

One

All her life, fourteen-year-old Mary Ann Whittaker's mother had lectured her about the deadly peril that awaited a foolish young lady who ventured onto the public streets unaccompanied.

In the winter afternoon twilight as Mary Ann attempted to fight off a burly thief determined to wrest her reticule from her, she reflected that it was just her luck that for the first time in recent memory her affectionate but bird-witted mother had been right about something.

Mary Ann wasn't entirely stupid; she had heard enough harrowing tales of what happened to careless solitary females to know the city streets could be dangerous. She intended to arrive in full sunlight, complete her transaction and be home again before her family discovered her missing. But she couldn't contrive to slip out of the house undetected as early as she hoped, and she had grossly underestimated the time it would take to walk here.

"Hand over your blunt, my pretty," Mary Ann's assailant growled, obviously surprised and annoyed that she was putting up such a spirited fight, "and you won't get hurt."

"Never," she said through gritted teeth as she landed a blow on his shoulder with her flailing fist. If he stole her only decent piece of jewelry before she could pawn it, all would be lost.

He was angry now. The expression in his beady, red-rimmed eyes told Mary Ann that while in the beginning he might have been content to amuse himself by terrorizing a cringing, helpless girl and stealing her valuables, now he would do her an injury if he could.

Panic gave strength and desperation to Mary Ann's grim struggle, but the thief soon succeeded in throwing her to the ground.

"Not so high and mighty now, are you, sweetheart?" he snarled. She could smell the stench of the garbage in the street and his foul breath against her face as she struggled to free herself of his pinioning arms.

"Let go of me!" she cried. Then she did something she had never done in her life. She opened her mouth and screamed at the top of her lungs. The man flinched and slapped her.

"That will be enough of *that,* missy," he said, grinning now that he had asserted his brutish superiority over her.

It was stupid of her to waste her hard-won breath on a scream. There had been people in the street when the man attacked her. None came to her assistance then, and none would now. Her injured cheek stung like fire, and this gave new life to her struggles. She had no wish to end her life in this horrible, dirty, smelly place at the hands of this brute. His weight crushed her. He was laughing now. Actually laughing!

Mary Ann felt tears start in her eyes. Her nose was running. He was going to murder her and throw her dead body into the filthy river. She just knew it! And her mother and sisters would never know what happened to her.

Her vision darkened as the man's thick fingers found her throat and tightened. Then, all at once, air rushed back into her lungs and the man's weight was suddenly removed from her body.

Blinking through tears of fright, Mary Ann looked up

into the face of what appeared to be an angry golden god framed in the glare of the setting sun. With cool efficiency, this startling apparition spun the gibbering thief around and struck him hard on the jaw. Then he grabbed the fellow by the collar of his coat and threw him bodily into the street.

"Be off with you," the golden man shouted after the thief, who had started scurrying away as soon as he hit the ground. The thief gave a backward look of pure, unadulterated terror and ran off.

"Did he hurt you, miss?" her savior asked as he tenderly assisted the stunned Mary Ann to her feet. She could only shake her head and stare into his wonderful face as she clung to his arm like a ninny. When she realized what she was doing, she let go and stepped back to pull herself together.

At first glance, her rescuer had seemed like a supernatural creature out of Greek mythology. Now she realized he was quite mortal.

He still looked like a golden god—all disheveled sun-streaked sandy hair, compelling eyes that shifted in color between amber and sea green, beautifully sculpted high cheekbones and wide shoulders. But now that she really looked at him, she realized her hero was a bit worse for wear. His coat, though tailored in what even a green girl like Mary Ann recognized as the first stare of fashion, was rumpled and could have used a good brushing; there was a rakish suggestion of stubble on his strong jaw.

The stubble would have made a lesser man look slovenly. It only made *him* look dashing. His face was tanned the handsome brown of the outdoorsman except for some little lines at the corners of his eyes, suggestive of squinting into the sun. Mary Ann could imagine him in armor, fighting dragons. Or in flowing shirt and leather scabbard fastened at his lean hips, defending a ship from pirates.

Under ordinary circumstances Mary Ann would find it painful even to *look* at him, the way she had found it painful to look at the exquisite hand painted dolls in the shops when she was a small girl. She knew instinctively that men so handsome—and dolls so expensive—were not for the likes of insignificant little Mary Ann Whittaker.

The stranger frowned and peered at her in concern.

"The blackguard *hit* you, did he?" he exclaimed, sounding outraged as he gently touched the place just under her cheekbone that pained her.

Mary Ann suddenly found her tongue.

"My reticule!" she cried.

"Here it is," he said, picking it up off the ground.

"Oh, thank heavens," she said with a sigh of relief as she clutched it to her chest. "Thank you, sir. I owe you an obligation I can never repay. If this had been lost, I—"

The thought was so horrible, she couldn't continue.

"A pleasure," he said solemnly. "What have you got in there, a fortune in gold?"

She smiled at him.

"My pearl ring. I was just going to pawn it."

"*You* were going into the pawnbroker's shop?" he asked in a tone of shocked disbelief. "Alone?"

Mary Ann couldn't help giving her savior a look of annoyance.

How like fate to send her a dashing hero who would begin to sound just like her mother and bossy older sisters after only a few moments' acquaintance. Mary Ann's existence was plagued with doomsayers whose only mission in life was to tell her what she could not do. It didn't mollify her in the least that in this instance they would have been right.

"Thank you again for your assistance, sir. I will trouble you no further," she said in a tone of voice meant to show him that she could take care of herself perfectly well. Now that the danger was past, she wanted nothing so much as to burst into tears of sheer reaction and weep all over his manly chest. She *refused* to make such a fool of herself.

"My good girl," he said kindly, "the number of dead

cats on the street should give you *some* indication that this is no place for a young lady. As soon as you are alone again, some other curst thief probably will come along to finish the job the first one started."

"I know I should have brought our maid," she admitted, "but she would have told my mother at once."

"Yes, there is that, Miss—" He paused and raised one eyebrow.

"Whittaker, sir. Mary Ann Whittaker," she said, offering her hand.

He accepted her hand, but merely held it as he stared intently into her face. Her skin tingled at his touch and she felt her cheeks flush with embarrassment. "Sir? Is something wrong?" she asked.

"No. Not at all," he said, giving her a crooked smile. "I had not realized at first how very young you are. You're a very brave girl."

Was that *admiration* shining in his eyes? For *her?* Any other adult of her acquaintance would have berated her for venturing into the city streets in an attempt to help her family, completely disregarding her good intentions.

And he had thought, at first, that she was *older.* How absolutely marvelous!

Mary Ann basked in his approval, but she felt compelled to tell the truth.

"I am not brave at all," she admitted, shamefaced. "It was cowardly of me to scream like that."

"Cowardly? No. Not after the way you outfaced a brute twice your size. With your permission, I will accompany you on your errand and see you home."

He was asking her *permission!* No one *ever* asked Mary Ann's permission. They just did as they pleased, and they expected her to adjust her behavior accordingly.

"You would do that? For me?" she asked, thrilled.

"With pleasure," the beautiful man said with a slight bow. "Let us have a look at this ring of yours. I will conduct the transaction for you, if you wish."

He was doing it again—treating her with respect. As the middle child in a family of five girls, no one *ever* treated Mary Ann with respect, or regarded her existence at all, for that matter, except as another mouth to feed.

At that moment, Mary Ann fell completely and irrevocably in love.

"How much do you think it will fetch?" she asked hopefully as she showed him the pearl ring. Papa had given it to her two years ago in one of his sporadic fits of generosity. That was before he gambled away his fortune and drank himself to death. "As much as ten pounds, do you think?"

The golden man took the ring in his hand and looked at it for too long. On his large, well-formed palm her greatest treasure looked utterly insignificant. Mary Ann felt a rush of panic. Were they not real seed pearls after all?

"Ten pounds is a lot of money," he said at last.

"I know," she said, feeling desperate. "But there are six of us, you see, and Mama will have no money until next quarter day. Ten pounds would settle our account with the butcher and buy a goose for Christmas dinner. My sister Lydia says we could live on it through the new year, if we are very frugal."

He gave her a look so full of compassion that she felt tears form in her eyes again.

"You must love your family very much to give this up," he said softly as he placed the ring in his breast pocket and offered his arm to escort her into the shop as if she were a grand lady instead of a scrubby schoolgirl.

Mary Ann relaxed.

The ring must be valuable after all.

Ten pounds. The girl would be lucky to get ten shillings for the pretty but insignificant piece of trumpery.

Lionel St. James felt an unaccustomed lurch in the region of his heart at the look of absolute trust in the girl's vulnerable brown eyes.

No one had looked at him like that in—well, no one had *ever* looked at him like that.

As he suspected, the pearl ring would have fetched far less than ten pounds, but he surreptitiously made up the shortfall from his own purse. Lady Luck had smiled upon him over the tables last night, and he was of a mind to be generous.

Inside the hackney carriage, Lionel St. James—who never paid the least attention to anybody—found himself listening intently while the girl artlessly poured out her whole sad history in a cheerful, matter-of-fact tone completely devoid of self-pity.

What a courageous little thing she is, Lionel thought, and what a tragedy it might have been if he hadn't happened along and seen the bully terrorizing her. She might even be dead by now. Pretty little Mary Ann Whittaker deserved a chance to grow up.

It certainly didn't take much to make her happy.

A goose for Christmas dinner. She asked nothing for herself—only for her family.

Well, Lionel would do his best for her.

Then he would leave her before he contaminated her like he had everything else that had been good in his life.

"Where have you been, you *wicked* girl!" shrieked Mary Ann's eldest sister, Vanessa, when the stranger handed her out of the hackney carriage. Right behind Vanessa was her next eldest sister, Lydia, glaring at Mary Ann with her mouth set in a straight line and her hands planted on her ample hips.

It was full darkness now, and from the looks of the shabby rented house, every candle in it had been lighted.

Mary Ann felt a moment of shame for frightening her sisters, but she could not be sorry. She ran to them at once and opened her reticule to show them the money it contained. They were speechless for a moment, and then Lydia grasped her by the shoulders.

"Mary Ann, you little wretch! What have you *done?* And who *is* that man?" Lydia demanded.

That was when Mary Ann realized that although the stranger had encouraged her to tell him her whole life's history, he had told her nothing at all about himself.

She turned to introduce her rescuer to her sisters, only to see that he had gotten back inside the carriage and was leaving her without even saying good-bye.

"Come back!" she called out.

"Mary Ann! A lady does not shout in the street," Vanessa said, looking scandalized. She put her arm around Mary Ann's shoulders to guide her into the house. "Mama has been having the vapors ever since we discovered you missing. How *could* you do such a thing?"

"But I don't even know his name," Mary Ann said plaintively.

"Never mind *him,*" Lydia said scornfully. "We must restore you to Mama at once or she will make herself sick with worry!"

Mama's face was stained with tears when Mary Ann went to her in the parlor. She threatened to lock her in her room until Judgment Day if she ever played such a cruel prank on her long-suffering mother again, but her eyes cleared magically when she saw the ten pounds.

"Mary Ann! My clever darling!" she cried. "Ten pounds! And for your pearl ring, too."

"Whoever would give so great a sum for that little ring?" Lydia asked with narrowed eyes. "And who *is* that man who brought you home?"

"I don't know," Mary Ann said tragically. "And now that you have scared him off, I may never find out."

Early on Christmas Eve morning a messenger delivered two parcels to Mary Ann. The first contained her precious pearl ring, and the second contained the biggest, freshest, fattest dressed goose any of them had ever seen, neatly cocooned in a wrapping of white paper.

Lydia cornered the messenger and questioned him, but he refused to divulge the identity of the ladies' benefactor. When Lydia and the maid went to the butcher shop with Mary Ann's windfall to pay their bill and buy a chicken for dinner, they found the debt mysteriously paid in full and the formerly surly butcher all flattering attention.

In celebration, Lydia and the maid went around to the shops and came back with all manner of wondrous things—even hothouse oranges for the younger girls and flowers for the table. On Christmas morning the shabby house was filled with the delicious fragrance of roasting goose.

They were all inclined to regard their good fortune as a Christmas miracle.

Amy and Aggie, Mary Ann's younger sisters, went wide-eyed with delight when they tasted their first bites of orange. Mama sang as she went about the house and didn't fall into the vapors even once for a whole week. Vanessa made a plum cake, and even Lydia temporarily reverted to the jolly girl she had been before financial ruin had forced her to bully them all into frugal habits.

The stranger's gift turned out to be a promise of better times to come.

Miraculously, the remains of the feast lasted until Mama's quarter day allowance came, and two years later Vanessa married a kind and handsome viscount whose chief pleasure in life was to provide every luxury for his mother-in-law and sisters-by-marriage.

Mama and Mary Ann's younger sisters often speculated that the stranger had been not a mortal man, but an angel come to give them courage in their time of trouble.

Not Mary Ann, though.

She knew the golden man was not an angel.

He was the man she was going to marry, even if it took her the rest of her life to find him.

Two

Mary Ann Whittaker flinched when her maid stuck another pin into her hair.

"That's *enough,* Monique," she snarled with mock ferocity. "You've been at it for *hours!*"

Mary Ann's little sisters, Aggie and Amy, ages eleven and twelve, were seated on the bed, giggling and carelessly rumpling the pretty muslin gowns they had donned for dinner as they offered Monique many helpful suggestions for Mary Ann's adornment. Monique cheerfully ignored them all.

"Don't be a baby," said Mary Ann's eldest sister, Vanessa, as she held up two perfectly ravishing evening gowns. "Do you fancy the green or the ivory for tonight, Mary Ann?"

Because she was a married lady, Vanessa wore a dashing gown of sapphire blue lace embroidered with sparkling beads that would have been deemed too sophisticated for an unmarried woman such as Mary Ann, even though Mary Ann, at one-and-twenty, thought she was getting rather long in the tooth for girlish muslins.

"The ivory," said Aggie, who thought herself quite the

fashion authority. *"Please,* Mary Ann," she added soul-fully.

"The green," Mary Ann said wryly. She smiled at Aggie's look of surprised reproach. As a rule, Mary Ann humored her sisters in such matters. "I'm sorry, love. Mama's orders. The ivory is to be saved for a grander occasion."

Aggie was silenced. In the all-important matter of dress, Mama's word was Law.

"Monique, I am going to turn you off without a character!" Mary Ann declared when another pin grazed her tender scalp.

"She doesn't mean it, Monique," Vanessa said kindly when Monique's hands froze above Mary Ann's head. Monique nodded and resumed her labors. With some indignation, Mary Ann realized the maid was trying not to smile.

Mary Ann dispassionately regarded her own face in the mirror.

"Your hair looks beautiful," Vanessa said, smiling, when Mary Ann's coiffure appeared to be firmly anchored on top of her head.

"I'll be the belle of the ball," Mary Ann prophesied as she made a twisted, bug-eyed face that caused Aggie and Amy to scream with laughter. Vanessa exchanged a look of long suffering with the maid.

Mary Ann had thought her ordeal over, but instead of standing back so she could rise and don her gown, Monique opened a box to reveal several artificial ivory roses with combs attached.

"See here, Monique," Mary Ann said in mock trepidation as she regarded the long, pointy teeth of those combs. "What do you imagine you are going to do with those?"

"Now, Miss Mary Ann," Monique murmured in gentle reproof as she began the process of securing the roses in Mary Ann's upswept hair. "The mistress's orders."

"More pins," Mary Ann wailed.

"You are going to look so pretty," Vanessa said. Her beautiful eyes were shining.

Mary Ann's heart swelled with love. Vanessa truly did believe these insipid ivory roses were going to transform her prosaic younger sister into a dainty fairy princess. But when Monique finished her handiwork, Mary Ann was surprised to see the roses *did* look well in her hair. She should have known. Mama was helpless when it came to running a household efficiently, but on matters of female adornment she was infallible.

"Now for the gown. Madame has outdone herself this time," Vanessa continued as she admired the genius of London's most expensive mantua-maker. It was a lovely confection. The skirt was covered with a gossamer layer of ivory net embroidered with delicate yellow flowers and green leaves around the hem. Puffs of more embroidered ivory net formed the sleeves.

All three of her sisters sighed with admiration when Monique settled the gown over Mary Ann's shoulders and hips. It fit perfectly, as well it should after the hours of fittings Mary Ann had endured. Not that she minded. The younger Mary Ann, who had worn her older sisters' cast offs, used to daydream about having a wardrobe of lovely gowns, all in the first stare of fashion. The reality was every bit as satisfying as she had imagined.

When Monique pronounced her ready, Mary Ann turned to examine her reflection in the long cheval glass.

As usual, she was a bit startled by the statuesque, dark-haired vision she saw there. Inexplicably, Annabelle Whittaker's plain middle daughter had turned into a beauty, and the carefully chosen green gown, while perfectly ladylike, made the most of Mary Ann's full-bosomed, narrow-waisted figure.

One would think the sight of Mary Ann in this guise would make the ambitious Mrs. Whittaker's heart swell with pride, yet when that exacting lady bustled into the room, she frowned as Mary Ann saluted, clicked her heels together and stood at mock attention before her for inspection.

In her mama's eyes, Mary Ann's lack of reverence toward the all-important matter of a lady's appearance was a serious defect in her character.

"What is this, miss?" Mrs. Whittaker demanded, indicating the offending slender golden chain as she adjusted the neckline of the gown to better display Mary Ann's shoulders and a discreet expanse of bosom. Aggie and Amy quietly filed out of the room. Although in general she was the most affectionate of mothers, Mrs. Whittaker's younger daughters knew she had little tolerance for girlish levity at such a time. "You know very well you are to wear the emerald pendant dearest Alexander bought you for your birthday."

Mary Ann withdrew the dainty pearl ring, long grown too small for even her littlest finger, from its usual resting place between her breasts.

"I wear it always," she said simply as she turned the bauble in her hand. "You know that, Mother."

Mrs. Whittaker put her hands on her hips.

"This sentimentality for your late papa's memory is all very well, my dear, but there *are* limits. I have always believed it better to please the living than the dead, and you would not want to hurt Alexander's feelings by spurning his gift."

Since Mary Ann could hardly tell her mother that the pearl ring was worn in remembrance, not of her late father but of the splendid stranger who had so gallantly come to her rescue seven years ago, she merely reached into the jewel box on her vanity and withdrew the dainty emerald pendant.

"It *is* pretty," she said, enjoying the green fire of the stone in the light. "I shall wear them both."

Of course, her mother wasn't pleased by this. The two chains together would make a very odd appearance, she protested. When Mary Ann added the pendant Mrs. Whittaker had to admit, though, that the shorter chain of the emerald that nestled beneath her collarbones framed by the longer chain of the ring tucked back inside the neckline of the gown was not displeasing.

"Now Mary Ann," her mother chided her, "I hope you are not going to spend all evening with your friends, gossiping and joking, instead of dancing. You don't want to scare the gentlemen away."

"Indeed, not," Mary Ann said dryly.

"I don't know what I am going to do with you," Mrs. Whittaker said in despair at Mary Ann's failure to consider the all-important subject of eligible gentlemen with the proper respect. "Alexander said you refused Lord Renfield. It was most embarrassing for him, for they are great friends."

"The gentleman is convinced that he is The Almighty's gift to all of womankind," Mary Ann said. "I am confident that his self-esteem will survive the disappointment."

"Could it be you have reason to expect a proposal from Sir Walter Burroughs?" she asked hopefully. "He was quite attentive to you at the ball last week. Now, if *he* offers for you—"

"He won't. He was only dancing with me to make Georgina Wingfield jealous."

Mrs. Whittaker sighed.

"I don't know what has gotten into you, Mary Ann," Mrs. Whittaker complained. "You used to be the most docile and obedient child."

Mary Ann merely smiled, remembering her first act of rebellion at the age of fourteen. If not for being assaulted and almost robbed, she wouldn't have met *him*. It had changed her life.

Since Mary Ann had attained her twentieth birthday

unwed, her mother had become increasingly frantic to find her a husband before she degenerated into an old maid. But to her mother's frustration and her brother-in-law's puzzlement, Mary Ann continued to instruct Alexander to decline every one of the flattering offers she had received since her come-out three years ago.

Like her elder sisters, Vanessa and Lydia, Mary Ann was determined to marry for love, and that meant she would have to wait for her kind, handsome, golden hero to return to her. If he never did, so be it. There were worse things than being a spinster—marriage to one of the infinitely boring young men who flocked to her side at balls, for instance.

She had been tempted a time or two—a girl *does* get weary of the awkwardness of being an unattached female, after all—but how could she live with herself if she married the wrong man and then *he* came back into her life?

Outwardly, she did what was expected of her without complaint. She wore the lovely gowns her mother bought with Alexander's money. She danced at balls and was polite to the gentlemen who flocked to her side. But in her heart of hearts, she continued to wait for *him*.

Mary Ann, as Mrs. Whittaker frequently told her, was every bit as stubborn as her provoking sister, Lydia, who had disappointed her ambitious mother by marrying a cavalry officer and following the wretched man wherever he and the 10th Royal Hussars led her instead of succumbing to the charms of the well-to-do country squire who had offered for her. Even now Lydia was in Scotland, darning her own stockings and cheerfully contriving to feed herself, her husband and their young son on an officer's pay without a shred of regret.

Mary Ann accepted her gloves and fan from Monique, gave her image a last look in the cheval glass and accompanied her mother to the drawing room.

"You look exquisite, Mary Ann," her brother-in-law,

Alexander Logan, Lord Blakely, reassured her after dinner when he positioned her between himself and Vanessa in the reception line for the ball. As the only son of the earl, Alexander was acting as a sort of secondary host.

Stoneham House was brilliant with candlelight and elegant decorations of holly and pine boughs interspersed with expensive red hothouse roses and satin ribbons. An elaborate kissing bough heavy with mistletoe, spiced apples and flowers was suspended from the ceiling. Satin ribbons in red and green festooned the bottom of the kissing bough and were secured at the four corners of the handsome, oblong room with more flowers.

It was the evening of the traditional pre-Christmas ball at Stoneham House, and all of polite society remaining in London would be expected to attend. Many of England's first families arranged their shopping excursions to the capital so they would still be in London for it. After the ball, Alexander would sweep his family-by-marriage off to his country house for the Blakelys' holiday house party. Last year Lydia enlivened this event by giving birth to her son, Quentin Alexander, right in the middle of it.

Weary of her mother's machinations to get her married, Mary Ann was looking forward to rusticating with her family for the rest of the winter. While she smiled and shook hands and dutifully presented her cheek to be kissed by various elderly ladies, Mary Ann anticipated the long, festive evening before her without much hope.

Lionel St. James handed his hat, evening cape and gloves to a hovering footman. He tensed when he saw Lord Blakely break off his conversation with a lavender-turbaned dowager and approach him with a look of surprise on his face—as well he might, since their primary acquaintance was over a gambling table at some of the least respectable clubs in town and it was unlikely in the extreme that one of London's most notorious gamblers numbered among the Earl of Stoneham's invited guests.

Lionel hadn't seen Blakely often in recent years—not since the viscount had settled down to become a respectable married man, actually.

By showing up at the ball uninvited, Lionel was gambling that by now Blakely was bored with domestic bliss and ready to resume some of London's congenial masculine pleasures—losing his blunt to Lionel, for instance. If so, he was more likely to be amused than offended by Lionel's presence, and he might be persuaded to meet Lionel in a friendly game of cards in the very near future. If the gods were truly kind, Blakely might bring along some of his rich friends.

An influx of the ready would be *most* welcome, for Lionel had pockets to let after a run of bad luck. Men who made their living at the gambling tables learned to expect such small reverses, but the timing was disastrous. Soon Blakely, like most of the well-heeled gentlemen of the ton, would leave London to spend Christmas and welcome the new year at his country house with his family, so the richest potential players would be out of Lionel's reach. Lionel had nothing to lose by reminding Blakely of the many convivial evenings they had spent at various gambling hells.

And if he managed to catch a glimpse of Blakely's sister-by-marriage, little Mary Ann Whittaker, all the better.

"St. James, old fellow," Blakely said with an amused quirk of one eyebrow. Lionel gave a sigh of relief. First hurdle crossed. "To what do I owe this unprecedented honor?"

It was as polite a way as any of asking him what the devil he was doing here.

Lionel matched his offhand tone.

"I hope you don't mind, Blakely. I was in the neighborhood and all that."

"Not at all. Do join me in a glass of wine," Blakely said graciously.

Lionel interpreted this as Blakely's little way of saying the wolf was welcome to the henhouse as long as he behaved himself—and he didn't intend to take his eyes off Lionel for a second until he left.

Fair enough.

Lionel hadn't attended a respectable society party like this in years—not since his conniving stepmother persuaded his father to disinherit him in favor of *her* son—and he saw these affairs had lost none of their stuffiness in his absence. His first objective—bringing himself to Blakely's attention—had been accomplished. In this crush of people, he realized, he was unlikely to achieve his second before Blakely politely showed him the door.

Lionel had known for a long time that Blakely had married the eldest Miss Whittaker, and little Miss Mary Ann had landed in clover with the rest of her family. Since Blakely's father was the Earl of Stoneham, Mary Ann was likely to be among the guests at the ball.

All Lionel wanted was a glimpse of the girl he had never forgotten. He needed to see that she was well and happy. The problem was, when he last saw her, she was an appealing child dressed in a well-worn, outgrown coat. Maybe that sweet memory would stop haunting him once he saw for himself that she had turned into a shallow, artificial society darling.

Scanning the room as Blakely escorted him through the ballroom with a seemingly friendly arm over his shoulder that was as confining as a steel band, Lionel decided that he probably wouldn't know her even if he saw her. She was bound to have changed a great deal in seven years.

Then the current dance ended and sudden recognition dawned when he spotted a lovely dark-haired girl in profile as her clearly besotted partner took reluctant leave of her.

Lionel realized he had been mistaken. He would have known her anywhere.

He stopped abruptly and stared, which caused Blakely to trip over his own feet with a stifled exclamation of annoyance.

The girl's profile was delightful with its upturned nose and decidedly firm chin. Her gown seemed to float around her graceful figure, and her thick, luxurious dark brown hair was crowned with roses. She regarded her partner with a tolerant smile on her face as the ardent gentleman kissed her fingers. The man was so young it was painful. Had *he* ever been that young?

Then, as if she could feel him staring at her, she turned and looked right into Lionel's bemused eyes.

He had thought her lovely before, but now she was positively radiant.

Life sprang into her big brown eyes and made them shine with pleasure. Her cheeks flushed with a pink glow, and she approached him with her graceful arms extended as if she intended to embrace him.

Lionel and Blakely both glanced surreptitiously behind them to see who she was looking at, but Mary Ann solved the mystery by walking right up to Lionel and taking both of his hands in hers.

He risked a look at Blakely and saw how his eyes had narrowed in displeasure.

"I am so glad you came tonight," Mary Ann said, looking up adoringly into Lionel's face.

To his embarrassment, he couldn't say a word. He just returned the pressure of her hands in his and let her lead him into the waltz that had just begun.

At last, Mary Ann thought, delirious with happiness, when the man she had waited for all these years put his arm around her waist and clasped her trembling right hand in his firm, warm one. Mary Ann's heart was beating so fast and so loudly that she was surprised it didn't throw the other dancers off tempo.

Her golden hero had returned.

He was a little less golden now. His hair was still fair, but it contained none of the blond sunstreaks she had remembered. His eyes were still sea green with amber lights in them. He had been handsome in rumpled wool the day she met him seven years ago; in black evening clothes and crisp white linen, he was devastating.

She had been right to wait for him. Her mind raced ahead to their wedding. She would rather wed immediately, but it was such a hardship for the guests to travel in winter. She would wait until spring, she decided, and not a moment longer. That would give her just enough time to complete the fittings for her trousseau.

Mary Ann enjoyed an intoxicating daydream of herself, dressed in white with a lush bouquet of pink roses and white orchids in her gloved hand as she looked up at Lionel through her lashes.

"Miss Whittaker, I suspect you have mistaken me for someone else," said Lionel when he at last found his tongue. Her perfume filled his senses with the scent of apple blossom.

Her laugh was like the music of church bells.

"Hardly! You are the gentleman who rescued me from that horrid thief and redeemed my ring, are you not? How could you think I would forget you?"

To his annoyance, he was speechless again. His usual careless savoir faire in his dealings with the fair sex utterly deserted him.

The movement of the dance showed him Blakely's thunderstruck countenance. His host was now accompanied by two ladies, a very pretty brunette and a diamond-bedecked matron who looked as if she might have an apoplexy at any moment. From her resemblance to Mary Ann, he thought the brunette was probably Blakely's wife. The matron was unmistakably Lady Letitia Logan, his formidable aunt and one of the doyennes of high society. From the expression on her face, she might have discovered a rat gnawing at the hem of her skirt.

It was highly unlikely now that Lord Blakely and his well-heeled friends would oblige Lionel with the game of cards Lionel so desperately needed to replenish his empty pockets. Even the most easygoing gentleman drew the line firmly at permitting a scapegrace such as Lionel to associate with a young female member of his family.

Lionel would be fortunate, indeed, to avoid the indignity of being escorted from the room by the Earl of Stoneham's footmen and thrown out into the street.

He gave a mental shrug. The pleasure of waltzing with the delightful Miss Whittaker would be well worth the humiliation.

One dance, he promised himself. *Then I will get out of her life forever.* Her protective brother-in-law would see to it, if he did not.

"Will you tell me your name?" she asked, oblivious to the fate that awaited him.

"Lionel St. James," he said with a solemn inclination of his head, "at your service, Miss Whittaker." *At least until Blakely throws me out of here,* he added mentally.

Mary Ann brightened.

"Are you related to Melissa St. James? I like her excessively. In fact, she would be here tonight if her family had not gone abroad."

Melissa. His little half-sister.

He had read in the society columns that Sir Andrew St. James and his family were spending the winter in southern Italy or he never would have risked coming anywhere near a *ton* party.

"No. No relation at all," he said without a single twinge of conscience. It was even true, in a way. His father and stepmother had made it perfectly clear that he was to have no further contact with them or either of his half-siblings after tarnishing their name with the scandal that was on everyone's lips ten years ago.

If they were so determined to deny him, he was only honoring their wishes when he returned the favor.

"There is a resemblance, so I wondered," Mary Ann said thoughtfully.

"A mere coincidence," he said.

"We tried to discover your identity after your kindness to us, but the messenger refused to divulge it. I don't know how we can repay you for your generosity."

"Anyone else would have done the same. Pray do not regard it."

"How kind you are, and how modest," she said, giving his hand a squeeze. "Well, now that I have found you again, you must meet my mother and sister."

"Some other time, perhaps," he said wryly as the dance wound to a close, and he saw that Blakely had made it his business to be waiting at Lionel's elbow when it did.

Mary Ann greeted her brother-in-law with an innocent smile of pleasure.

"Alexander! You will never guess who this gentleman is!"

"Mr. St. James and I are well acquainted," Blakely said grimly. No doubt he was remembering the many nights of deep play during which Lionel had relieved him of most of his allowance and army pay.

"Alexander, you do not understand," Mary Ann said, clearly taken aback by her brother-in-law's less-than-cordial tone. She lowered her voice. "Mr. St. James is the kind gentleman who redeemed my ring and sent us a Christmas goose seven years ago when we were in despair."

Her expression indicated that she expected Alexander to clasp Lionel to his bosom like a long-lost brother.

Instead, Blakely clapped him on the shoulder and gave Mary Ann a stiff smile.

"Is he, indeed?" he said pleasantly. "Come along, Mr. St. James. We are long overdue for a talk."

Inexorably, he escorted Lionel away from Mary Ann, whose expression was anxious as she watched them go.

"You will dance with me again, will you not?" she called after him.

"Regrettably, no," Lionel said, acknowledging the unmistakable message in Blakely's eyes. "I have another engagement this evening, I fear."

Once they were across the threshold of the card room, Blakely relaxed his grip and gave Lionel a wolfish smile.

He shook his head in warning when Lionel swept the room full of card players with a speculative eye. Lionel shrugged philosophically and took the chair Blakely indicated.

"All right, old fellow," Blakely said in a low, menacing voice as he poured them both a glass of port. "What is this nonsense about you being the saintly benefactor who rescued them from starvation all those years ago?"

"Well, it's true," Lionel said, quailing a bit. "I saw this little girl being throttled by a bully, and the next thing I knew I was pulling him off her."

"You?" Blakely scoffed. "Coming to the aid of a damsel in distress? A *poor* damsel in distress? Tell me another!"

"Wasn't quite myself," Lionel murmured. Blakely *would* stare if he knew how Lionel still cherished the memory of that courageous little girl's innocent face and worshipful eyes.

Blakely gave a snort of disbelief.

"Wonderful. Now Mary Ann thinks you're some sort of knight in shining armor. I hope I need not tell you that I will disabuse her of that notion *immediately*. Nothing personal, you understand. You're the best of companions, Lionel, when a man is looking for a bit of sport, but I can't have you associating with Mary Ann. I'm afraid I will have to ask you to leave as soon as you finish your wine."

"In your shoes, I'd do the same," Lionel admitted with perfect honesty.

"Excellent. We understand one another."

The conversation then turned to sporting events and horseflesh, and Lionel left Stoneham House on terms of perfect accord with his host, certain that he would never see the lovely Mary Ann Whittaker again.

Three

Lionel shrugged into the slightly threadbare dressing gown his man held for him and raised his brows in annoyance at the persistent knocking at the street door of his lodgings.

"Get rid of whoever that is, will you, Garland?" Lionel said as he seated himself in his leather chair and raised a cup of steaming black coffee to his lips.

"At once, sir," his manservant said, advancing purposefully to the door.

Lionel yawned. He had returned home last evening rather early for him, but his usually dreamless slumbers were interrupted by visions of the lovely Miss Whittaker. It had been a mistake to seek her out, an error he had no intention of repeating. His bad luck at the tables continued when he left Stoneham House for one of his favorite gambling hells. Seeing her again had not rid him of an obsession; it had only ruined his concentration.

Avoiding her in the future should not prove difficult, he reflected wryly; they hardly moved in the same circles.

Unfortunately for his resolve, at that moment the determined young lady herself marched into the room with Lionel's flustered manservant in her wake.

"See here, miss," the scandalized Garland said in a tone of deep disapproval. "You cannot disturb my master at this hour."

"Mr. St. James," Mary Ann said, smiling beatifically at Lionel, "please forgive the intrusion. I had to see you."

Lionel stood so abruptly in shock at the sight of her that he spilled the steaming contents of his coffee cup inside the front of his dressing gown and scalded his bare chest.

"Oh! I did not mean to startle you! Are you hurt?" she cried in distress, and ran across the room to him.

"Not at all," Lionel said as his eyes filled with unmanly tears and he strove very hard not to whimper. Incredibly, the girl reached for the collar of his dressing gown as if she would ascertain his injury for herself. An innocent young lady would naturally assume he was wearing shirt and pantaloons beneath his dressing gown at this hour of the day, which he definitely was not!

"Here, stop that!" he said in alarm, pushing her hands away before she learned the shocking truth for herself. To his dismay, the look of concern in her warm brown eyes made him want to cover those graceful French kid-gloved fingers with kisses instead.

Mary Ann was wearing a stylish blue merino pelisse trimmed with white fur that made the most of a delicate English rose complexion. Her cheeks were pink with cold.

The mere sight of all this fresh-faced loveliness made Lionel feel as if he were a hundred years old. He was painfully aware that he had not yet combed his hair or shaved, and his slippers were a trifle shabby.

His lodgings were no fit place for a lady. Although Garland struggled heroically to keep the place tidy, there was no hiding the fact that Lionel's worldly possessions were old and not in the best repair. An ancient horsehair divan of an indeterminate color between brown and gray and a threadbare carpet were the room's only furnishings except for the good leather chair—purchased years ago in an excess of optimistic extravagance from his first large gambling purse—and a scarred table. Mercifully, the yet unmade bed was hidden from the young lady's view by a screen. Garland's neat darns in the linens were all too apparent.

Soon after he purchased the leather chair, Lionel learned the painful truth that a professional gambler could easily starve if he squandered his blunt on domestic comfort. It was essential that Lionel support a gentlemanly appearance in matters of dress and horse because he made it his personal policy to gamble only with rich men who could afford to lose to him, but he neglected his lodgings shamefully. This didn't bother him overmuch until he saw Mary Ann's quickly suppressed expression of dismay.

Lionel took great care that none of his acquaintances had occasion to see his seedy lodgings. He felt humiliated and exposed that *she* should see them.

"Why have you come here?" he demanded. "If your loving brother-in-law finds out about this day's work, my girl, it will be grass before breakfast for me."

"He says I must not see you again," she said, looking troubled.

"You should listen to him."

"No! You must not say that," she said. There was no mistaking the hero worship in her eyes.

Blast it!

He was trying to do the right thing, and she was arguing with him. Well, it was time for the notorious Lionel St. James to put an end to her romantic delusions.

He seized her shoulders roughly and loomed over her.

Her eyes were wide as saucers as he advanced; she retreated until her back thumped against the wall.

He bent so his lips were inches away from hers.

"So, you want to discharge your crushing obligation to me, do you, little girl?" he asked with a mocking smile.

She nodded once and swallowed hard. It was plain she was too alarmed to speak.

"Good," he grated out, and kissed her with all the pent-up frustration in his blackened heart.

From the first touch of her soft lips, he realized how much he had longed to taste them. Instead of savoring, though, he ravaged, abrading her delicate skin with his rough whiskers. His senses filled with the apple blossom scent she used to adorn her person.

He probably smelled of stale sweat and sour claret.

They were both breathing hard when he ended the kiss. Her lips were swollen and her eyes were filled with hurt tears. He would cheerfully have taken ten lashes for every one of them.

Lionel waited stoically for her to slap him soundly in retribution for his abominable behavior. He braced himself for the pain.

To his despair, she moaned and put her graceful hands on his shoulders for support. She took a long, shuddering breath, like a disappointed child in need of comforting.

Lionel longed to cup her pretty face in his hands and place gentle kisses on her eyelids.

Instead, he stepped back.

"There," he said, as he allowed his lips to twist in a mocking travesty of a smile. "The debt is canceled. Go home, Miss Whittaker. This is no place for you."

Eyes huge in her stricken face, the girl turned and fled from the house.

"Good," Lionel said aloud, feeling like a blackguard as he heard the outside door slam shut.

Garland, who had been standing as if frozen in place throughout the whole disgraceful performance, suddenly came to life and poured more coffee into the cup.

"Will that be all, sir?" he asked with thinly veiled disapproval in his voice as he handed the cup to his master.

"Don't look at me like that," Lionel snapped. "I did

the decent thing and sent her away, so there's an end to it."

In that consoling thought, however, he was mistaken.

Mary Ann left Lionel St. James's lodgings with tears of humiliation running down her cheeks. Her lips felt swollen and abused.

She leaned outside the door for a moment, feeling shaken.

His mouth.

His arms.

This was not the kiss she had dreamed of all those years ago. There was nothing sweet or ardent about it. She gave, and he . . . took.

Like a ninny, she had run away from him as if all the devils in hell were after her.

Her dignity had suffered, but she was not defeated.

She took a deep breath and proceeded to the waiting carriage that contained her maid.

Lionel was trying to scare her away, of course. That brute who had crushed her in his arms was not *him*, but merely a part he was playing for her benefit. It was chivalrous of him to want to preserve her reputation from being damaged by association with him, but Mary Ann was made of sterner stuff than the typical milk-and-water miss.

Her mind had been made up from the moment she saw the virtual squalor in which he lived. His lodgings were even shabbier than the horrid rented house where she, her mother and her sisters had lived during that bleak year they were desperate. And Lionel did not have a loving family, as she did, to share his hardships.

Lionel had saved Mary Ann seven years ago when she was at wit's end, now *she* was going to save *him*.

Even Vanessa, who did not disobey her husband's expressed wishes lightly, did not hesitate. The Whittaker ladies were in the carriage practically before the tale was all the way out of Mary Ann's mouth.

Aggie was bouncing with excitement on the seat; Amy was trying very hard to act the part of a worldly young lady, but her eyes were shining with anticipation.

"Do you think he will come home with us right away?" Aggie asked.

"We are not going to give him any choice," Mary Ann replied. "We leave tomorrow to spend Christmas in the country, and he is going with us!"

"Alexander was very clear on the point that he does not wish for us to associate with Mr. St. James," Vanessa said, sounding conscience-stricken. "He is going to be very angry, I'm afraid."

"Vanessa, darling, Alexander is *not* the earth, moon and stars rolled into one," Mary Ann chided her. "Thunder does not crash when he speaks; lightning does not strike when he frowns. In other words, he can be *wrong.*"

"No one esteems dearest Alexander as much as I," Mama said, "but we *cannot* let poor Mr. St. James spend Christmas alone when we owe him so much."

She was right, of course. They all agreed on that.

As for Alexander, if Vanessa alone couldn't talk him around, the combined weight of all of them together would make short work of his objections. With all the confidence of ladies who knew themselves to be well loved, they proceeded to implement a plan that was as audacious as it was generous.

Lionel was just tying his neckcloth when a veritable army of handsome, well-dressed ladies in a variety of ages came marching into his lodgings, sweeping an affronted Garland ahead of them.

"I tried my best, sir," the little man said, absolving himself of blame.

"You had better save your breath for packing your master's clothes, my good man," the eldest lady said sternly. "Get to it, now. We leave tomorrow for Leicestershire."

"I do not believe I have had the pleasure, madam," Lionel said, frowning. Had she escaped from an asylum? He didn't know anyone in Leicestershire.

"Good day, Mr. St. James," she said pleasantly. "These are my daughters. We are taking you to my son-in-law's estate, where you will remain with us until the new year."

At that moment, he spotted Mary Ann, who had been half-hidden behind her mother as she bent to talk to one of a pair of young girls.

"Ah. Miss Whittaker," he said in a tone of resignation. "I see you have brought reinforcements."

One of the younger girls stepped forward and interrupted whatever Mary Ann was about to reply.

"Mr. St. James," she said, drowning him in innocent cornflower blue eyes, "you won't refuse to come with us, will you? Our Christmas will be *ruined* if you won't come."

"My sister Aggie," said Mary Ann, supplying the introduction he hadn't requested.

"Please," added the other girl soulfully.

"My sister Amy," Mary Ann said. Amy curtsied and smiled at him. Belatedly remembering her manners, young Aggie did the same.

"When we were little, we thought you were an angel," Amy said.

Lionel's mouth opened and closed in astonishment.

"There you have it, Mr. St. James," the older woman said, smiling. "Surely you would not ruin my children's Christmas. How could we not repay you for your kindness to us all those years ago?"

Lionel closed his eyes and took a deep breath. Mary Ann obviously had not seen fit to enlighten her mother on the crude nature of payment that he already had exacted from her, or Mrs. Whittaker would not be regarding him with so kindly an eye.

At a signal from their mother, the little girls came forward and each possessed herself of one of his hands.

"You do not fight fair, ma'am," he said wryly as he endured a double barrage of hopeful blue eyes.

She gave a brisk nod of triumph.

"Miss Whittaker. Ladies," Lionel said desperately. "I know you mean well, but Lord Blakely is going to . . ." He had been about to say "draw my claret," which just *proved* he had no business rubbing shoulders with respectable ladies. "Er, object strongly to my presence in his home. I assure you, I do not expect repayment from you for a simple act of kindness I performed for a child seven years ago."

The pretty brunette whom he assumed was Lady Blakely spoke up.

"It is not just Alexander's home, but *mine* as well," she said as blue fire danced in her fine eyes. "And I shall invite anyone I choose to visit it."

"Bravo, Vanessa!" Mary Ann cheered. "That's the spirit!"

Mrs. Whittaker gave her eldest daughter an approving nod and Mary Ann a quelling look.

"I'm sorry, ladies. It is quite impossible," Lionel said firmly.

"Nonsense," Mrs. Whittaker sniffed. "We can't permit you to spend the holiday *here*. Unless"—she paused to give him an uncertain look—"you planned to spend Christmas with your own family."

"I have no family, ma'am," he said, and was nonplussed when five pairs of female eyes instantly misted in sympathy. Blast! "I will not mind being alone, truly. I assure you, it would be best if I stay here—"

"Where you will spend Christmas all alone, drinking

yourself into a stupor, I suppose," Mary Ann said, sounding testy.

"Why not?" he retorted. "It sounds like the *perfect* holiday to me."

But he had lost, and he knew it.

Four

Lord Blakely scowled at the gentleman seated in the place of honor on the sofa in his drawing room. Aggie and Amy were seated on either side of him, looking as if manna from heaven dropped from the man's lips. Even more vexing, Mary Ann was positively radiant, although she, at least, had the decorum not to practically sit on his lap.

The emotion uppermost in Alexander's breast was jealousy. The younger girls usually looked at *him* like that.

Tonight they hardly glanced in his direction when he walked into the room.

"Is it not lovely, Alexander?" the mother of his twin sons said with a martial gleam in her eye when he approached that cheeky bas—, er, *bounder*, Lionel St. James, with every intention of grasping him by the collar and throwing him out of his house. "Mr. St. James will be joining us in the country for Christmas."

Alexander had opened his mouth to disabuse his cherished helpmeet of this ridiculous notion when Aggie smiled at him.

The little girl looked so trusting and so happy. Alexander looked around the room at the pretty, pink-cheeked, dark-haired ladies he loved so much. They were all dressed with special care, presumably in honor of their guest—a gentleman whom Blakely fervently wished to Perdition.

None of them had ever received anything but kindness at Alexander's hands, and they never would. Not while he had breath left in his body.

"Lovely," Alexander agreed with a stern look at the interloper. He gritted his teeth when Vanessa took St. James's arm and permitted him to lead her into the dining room.

"I can hardly wait to go into the country," Mary Ann said with sparkling eyes as Alexander escorted her, as the next eldest lady present, into the dining room. Mrs. Whittaker was dining out with several of her friends. "Do we have an extra pair of adult ice skates Mr. St. James may borrow?"

"I believe Vanessa has purchased several pairs for the use of guests," Alexander said.

"Oh, good!"

"This enthusiasm for the country is quite a new thing for you, my girl," Alexander couldn't help observing. "I remember last year you were reluctant to leave your friends to honor us with your presence."

"This year is special," she said with a glowing look at St. James's back. "How wonderful it will be to share Christmas with the gentleman who was so kind to us when we were desperate. It is my dream come true."

A dream, he scoffed inwardly. *A nightmare, more likely!*

Alexander was vexed when he observed the way Mary Ann rushed to take the seat at their guest's right, which made Amy and Aggie sulk a bit at being deprived of the privilege of sitting beside the interloper. The younger girls were on their best behavior this evening, which should have pleased Alexander but didn't. In any other circumstance, Aggie would have complained loudly at having her usual place appropriated by Mary Ann. It just showed how firmly the gamester had pulled the wool over his ladies' eyes.

At least St. James had the wit to look sheepish rather

than triumphant. A gloating look might well have earned him a facer as soon as the ladies retired from the table.

"I hope you like mutton, Mr. St. James," Vanessa said pleasantly when Lionel held her chair for her at the foot of the table.

"Very much, Lady Blakely," he said. The delicious aromas wafting from the doorway, where liveried staff members awaited the signal to serve the meal, had his mouth watering. As his luck at the tables decreased, so did the number of decent meals that found their way into his stomach. When it came between a good meal for himself and the board fees at a nearby stable for his horse, Lionel was inclined to defer to his horse.

The table was covered with a lace cloth over snowy linen, and twin silver candelabra cast a soft glow on the pretty, feminine faces surrounding him. All the ladies wore filmy gowns in soft pastel colors. They looked like they were made of spun sugar.

Lionel hoped when the food arrived he would not disgrace himself by bolting it down.

And he sincerely hoped that Lord Blakely, who was giving him a wolfish grin that boded ill for his continued good health, would allow Lionel to explain that he had been virtually abducted by the ladies before he smashed his fist into his jaw.

Later, as Lionel savored the taste of the mint jelly accompanying the mutton on his tongue, he didn't know whether he would be disappointed or relieved by a reprieve, if it should be forthcoming, from joining Lord Blakely's family party over the holidays.

When he left his father's house, he vowed that he would never enter his home again, and he had meant it. He was done with the hypocrisy of domestic tyranny. His father ruled his family with an iron fist, and Lionel could remember meals during which he could not swallow a bite because of his father's sarcastic jibes and his mother's silent tears. Lionel faced a humiliating scold and banishment from the meal if he made an unwise remark or spilled something at table.

His father's second wife did not suffer in silence, for her tongue was just as acidic as her husband's. When his stepmother permanently banished Lionel from her table during his rebellious adolescence because, she insisted, she could not endure the sight of him while she was eating, he gladly took all his meals with his old governess or, as soon as he was old enough, out of the house altogether.

As an adult Lionel soon discovered that his father's home was not unusual, for the veneer of civility married couples cultivated so carefully in public inevitably broke down at their own dinner table. Before he earned the censure of society, Lionel had endured countless dinner parties in which the host and hostess sniped at each other with insincere little smiles on their faces, as if that convinced *anyone* that they were merely teasing. If being disinherited had any beneficial result, it was his exclusion from such uncomfortable affairs.

But Lord Blakely's dining room table was much different. A child could see Blakely objected to Lionel's presence in his home, but he forbore to take it out on the women. The meal was surprisingly . . . pleasant.

The ladies did not quake in expectation of a rebuke from their lord and master. On the contrary, they chatted excitedly about their expectations for the holiday—the parties they would host and attend in their country neighborhood, the delicacies they would order for their guests' refreshment, the sleigh rides they would enjoy in the moonlight.

When Aggie, the youngest, accidentally dropped her spoon, no one paid the least attention except for a liveried footman who stepped forward to supply another. The girl thanked the footman with a pretty smile. At Lionel's family home, none of the family paid the least notice to an inferior who did them a service. To do so, his father maintained, was undignified.

In spite of his precarious position, Lionel found himself looking forward to the house party in Leicestershire. Throughout the years of his estrangement from his family he had maintained that such parties were devilish dull, but it would be no bad thing, now that he thought about it, for Garland and himself to rusticate for a bit. The tradesmen had been dunning them by post and in person for the payment of his bills. After the holiday, Lionel might well have to submit to the tender mercies of the cents-per-cent, but for now he could postpone the inevitable in comfort at Lord Blakely's expense.

Lionel had to smile when the liveried footman placed the sweet before him.

It was such a dainty thing—some sort of light, fluffy cake with a candied fruit sauce and cream on top. At the gentlemen's club and inns that Lionel frequented, the sweet consisted of hearty slabs of cake or pie unless it was dispensed with altogether in favor of gin or port. His father would have loudly demanded to know why there was a powder puff on his plate if either of his wives had possessed the temerity to expect him to eat such a thing.

Lord Blakely dipped his spoon into the confection with every appearance of enjoyment. Lionel followed suit, and it was so delicious he had to restrain himself from tipping the rest of the bowl into his mouth at once.

Crystal dishes full of fruited jellies and creams appeared on the table as well, all of them as insubstantial as air. Ladies' fare, Lionel's father would have contemptuously dismissed them. Lady Blakely pressed a taste of each one upon Lionel, and he was pleased to comply.

His indulgence in the sweets filled Lionel with such contentment that he almost missed his cue to rise and bow to the ladies as they took their leave.

"Don't be long, my darling," Lady Blakely said softly to her husband as she caressed his shoulder in passing. Without the least self-consciousness, Blakely took her hand and placed a fleeting kiss upon it. The look the couple exchanged told Lionel why marriage had put an end to Blakely's evenings at his club. He was very much in love with his wife, even after several years of marriage.

The poor devil.

When Blakely resumed his seat, he gave Lionel a look that quite took the smirk off his face.

"You may thank my wife and her sisters for the fact that you are sipping wine at my table instead of picking yourself up from the gutter on the street outside," he said pleasantly. "If you do anything—*anything*—to hurt them, I will personally cut out your liver and feed it to your own horse."

Lionel merely raised his eyebrows at him.

It cut both ways.

Blakely cared far more than was wise for the good opinion of his wife and sisters-in-law. No matter how much Lionel annoyed him, Blakely could not retaliate without bringing down their reproaches upon his own head.

However, Lionel did not make the grave error of attributing the viscount's threat to mere bluster. He *would* cut out Lionel's liver if he harmed them. Of this he had no doubt.

"It behooves us as gentlemen to come to an understanding," Blakely said as he sat back in his chair and gave Lionel a speculative look. "It appears to be important to Vanessa and her sisters that you accompany us to Leicestershire, so I will not object."

"Good of you," Lionel said with one upraised brow.

"I will not object," Blakely repeated, *"if* you will assure me that you will not in any way take advantage of Mary Ann's misguided infatuation for you."

Lionel felt his jaw clench at the implied insult.

"What do you take me for, Blakely?" he said bitterly. "I don't seduce innocents."

"Perhaps not. But you might be under the impression that you might marry one."

Lionel gave a bitter snort.

"I have no delusions about my prospects with respect to your precious sister-in-law, thank you very much," he said. "Do you think *I* want to give up my freedom to live under the cat's paw? We were friends once, Blakely. You should know better than that."

"Good. Just so there is no misunderstanding, I am prepared to pay you five hundred pounds if—"

Lionel's brows drew together.

"What are you saying?" he demanded.

"If you promise to stay with us for the duration of the house party, act the part of a model guest and disappear from Mary Ann's life when it ends."

Lionel's mouth dropped open.

"Confound it, Blakely," Lionel protested with a harsh laugh of derision. "You sound like the villain in a bad play!"

Blakely's narrowed gaze did not waver.

"St. James, if there is anything I have *ever* respected about you except for your skill at cards, it is your love for plain speaking. Do *not* disappoint me."

"Very well," Lionel said coolly. "Then I'll speak plainly and say I'm astonished a monkey is all you're willing to pay to save your innocent blossom from my evil clutches."

Dash it! Now *Lionel* sounded like the villain in a bad play! He half expected Blakely to say so, but the viscount was too intent upon his objective to notice the irony.

"Very well," Blakely said with a curt nod, as if he had been expecting this. "A thousand, then."

"A thousand," Lionel repeated, staring unflinchingly at Blakely with the carefully neutral expression he had so successfully cultivated as one of the most valuable tools in his arsenal as a gamester.

When it came to bluffing, Lionel was a master.

"Two thousand, then!" Blakely said, swallowing the bait.

Lionel permitted himself a small smile.

As he had intended, Blakely took this as a signal that his terms had been accepted.

"Excellent," Blakely said, reaching for his glass of port.

Lionel could hear the viscount's thoughts as clearly as if he had spoken them aloud.

He would have paid more.

Much more.

Lionel must be losing his touch.

No matter.

Two thousand pounds would settle the more pressing of his debts and provide a small stake until he could replenish his accounts at the tables. He did not worry about being turned out of his lodgings in the dead of winter for his own sake, but Garland had suffered enough indignity at his hands. Once the bloody holiday was over, Britain's richest and most influential men would return to London preparatory to taking their seats in Parliament, and Lionel would be waiting for them.

It galled him to accept money from Blakely, but, hell, he was filthy rich. The viscount could well afford to ensure Lionel's good behavior with a princely bribe.

The joke was on Blakely.

The two thousand pounds made not the slightest difference in Lionel's plans with regard to the delectable Mary Ann. She had been entirely safe from him all the time.

Not because Blakely would challenge Lionel to a duel and put a bullet through his chest if he even *thought* about trifling with the girl, but because it would be less painful to keep his distance than to watch her hero-worship of him turn to bitter disillusionment.

Five

Lionel was wont to travel lightly through life, so he stood, quite thunderstruck, on the threshold of Lord Blakely's town house as he watched the pandemonium that ensued when five adults and four children with their various servants and possessions removed themselves to the country for a month's stay.

He was almost embarrassed that all he had to convey there was one battered dressing case, his elderly manservant and his horse. Garland had been so proud to take his place in the second carriage with Lord Blakely's butler and valet, and Lady Blakely's and Mrs. Whittaker's maids.

Lionel felt a twinge of conscience. Garland had chosen to follow Lionel into exile from his father's house, and he uncomplainingly shared Lionel's hardships over the years when his skill and experience qualified him for a much more desirable situation. Lionel was uncomfortably aware that his horse often enjoyed better accommodations than his manservant.

Garland's simple pleasure in hobnobbing below stairs in a gentleman's residence with the other upper servants smote Lionel in a way that constant complaints never could have. The manservant's years of drudgery on Lionel's behalf must have been very lonely.

Mary Ann, calmly directing the bestowal of her gowns and maid, looked up at him with a twinkle in her lovely eyes.

"You slept well, I trust, Mr. St. James," she said cheerfully.

Lord Blakely had been watching a groom walk his horse, but now he came to attention and gave Lionel a warning look.

No doubt he disapproved of his sister-in-law's interest in their guest's sleeping habits.

Lionel couldn't help but sigh. That reckless good fellow, Captain Logan, as Blakely was known before he resigned his commission in a crack cavalry regiment, had degenerated into a prudish patriarch.

It was pitiful. Absolutely pitiful.

Mary Ann looked enchanting this morning in emerald green merino wool with a matching bonnet tied under the chin with rich satin ribbons. Rich brown fur trimmed the collar and cuffs of her costume, and her gloves and half-boots were made of leather that looked as soft as butter.

"Lady Blakely's servants have made me very comfortable, I thank you," Lionel said, tipping his hat to the young lady. He was tempted to inquire after her night's repose in return, just to annoy Blakely, but he decided he'd really rather not learn from personal experience whether Blakely was as handy with his fives as his fame at Gentleman Jackson's salon would seem to indicate.

Mary Ann stroked his horse's head approvingly.

"Aren't you the gorgeous fellow," she crooned. "What is his name?"

"Thunder," said Lionel. "Careful, Miss Whittaker. He's a bit restive this morning. He's not accustomed to standing about when he leaves the stable."

"I can see you're a high-spirited fellow," Mary Ann said to the horse. "Not like Alexander's old slug, Midnight."

"This old slug," Blakely said with perfect good humor as he reached out to caress his horse's back, "carried me throughout the war and endured several transports through stormy seas without complaint. Not quite ready for retirement yet, are we, old fellow?"

The stallion might be a bit past his prime, but he still looked to be a handful for a less than masterful horseman. Blakely's Midnight was, like Thunder, dancing in his impatience to be off.

Blakely gave a sigh of long suffering and patted Midnight's back again.

"Sorry old fellow," he said ruefully. "It will be at least another half hour—if we're lucky."

Despite their mutual mistrust, he and Lionel shared a heartfelt look of commiseration.

Lionel had stayed up much too late in his luxurious room, thinking and imbibing from the crystal decanter of spirits his hosts had thoughtfully provided to him. Gone were the days when he could indulge freely and not pay for it the morning after. His head ached like the very devil, and Garland's uncharacteristic morning chatter about the comforts of Lord Blakely's town house below stairs had grated on his nerves.

Lionel had given Garland a sharp recommendation to keep his raptures to himself that he now regretted. He was impatient to shake the cobwebs from his head with a brisk ride, but it would be some time, apparently, before the procession to Leicestershire would depart.

For *this,* Lionel had roused himself from a warm, comfortable bed at dawn—an hour he had not willingly witnessed in many a year.

He declined the services of the groom Blakely ordered to walk his horse for him and did the task himself, mostly to avoid further cheery morning conversation. Foiling this purpose, Blakely took his own horse in hand and walked the breadth of the yard along with him.

The high-pitched, excited squeals of Lord and Lady Blakely's twin sons and the agitated barking of their large, over-friendly dog made Lionel cringe. Servants were walking briskly, as if in the lockstep of a stately dance, from the house to the carriage with trunks and hot bricks and hampers of food for the travelers' sustenance. One of the twins noticed a favorite toy missing and began screeching at the top of his lungs. All preparations for departure halted as a frantic search ensued among the trunks in the third coach that contained the children's nursery staff and clothing.

Lord Blakely, who optimistically had hoped to leave two hours ago, looked back at the ensuing chaos stoically.

"Ah, the joys of traveling to the country with a family," Lionel said with a glimmer of satisfaction at Blakely's wry face. "If our old companions at Boodle's could see you now . . ."

Amazingly, Blakely gave Lionel a pitying look, as if he could look into Lionel's heart and see the emptiness there.

"The happiest day of my life was the day I married Vanessa," Blakely said simply. "The second happiest was the day my sons were born."

"Very affecting," Lionel said with a snort of skepticism. "But my father used to mouth just such platitudes in public as well, and life under his roof was hardly a testament to sweet domesticity."

"I saw your father and mother in London when Parliament was in session," Blakely said a bit too casually.

Lionel compressed his lips in annoyance. His past was none of Blakely's business—or anyone's, even though all the world had heard about the sordid scandal that brought about his estrangement from his family. He could have kicked himself by giving Blakely an opening to what was, for him, an excruciatingly painful subject.

"Stepmother," Lionel corrected him automatically, surprised that the word came out in three perfectly normal syllables. He half expected it to catch fire as it left his mouth, making his breath burn everything in his path, like that of a dragon.

"As you say," Blakely agreed. "They looked well."

"I didn't ask," Lionel said pointedly.

"Melissa made her come-out the same year as Mary Ann. She is a fine young woman."

"Damnation, Blakely!" Lionel spat out. "This is none of your business!"

It was all he could do not to ask about Julian, the half brother who had taken his place as his father's heir. Blakely might have sensed this, or maybe he just wanted to annoy him further.

"Your brother—I beg your pardon, St. James, your *half brother—seems to be a most conscientious young man.*"

Lionel gritted his teeth in annoyance.

"I do *not* wish to have this conversation with you."

"As you please," Blakely said. He looked as if he would like to say something more, but at that moment one of his sons, whose small body formed a perfect globe in his protective layers of warm clothing, ran up to Blakely on stubby legs and held his arms up in an unmistakable demand to be picked up. A plump nursemaid arrived, panting, behind the child.

"Got away from you, did he, Maisie?" Blakely said to the girl with one lifted eyebrow as he picked up the child and held him aloft in his arms. The little boy gave a squeal of delight that made Lionel flinch.

The girl blushed crimson at the subtle shading of disapproval in Blakely's otherwise perfectly pleasant voice. A yard full of tramping horses eager for a run was *not* a safe place for a three-year-old's caretaker to relax her vigilance.

"Beg pardon, your lordship," she said, bobbing a little curtsy. "He bolted without any warning, and—"

"Very well, Maisie," Blakely interrupted, looking at the girl. The child put both his chubby palms on Blakely's cheeks to turn his father's attention back to himself. "No harm done *this* time. You may come for him in a moment." Obviously relieved to be getting off with so mild a reprimand, the girl ran back to the head nurse.

"Papa! You must ride in the coach with us!" the child demanded.

"Not today, Jeremy, my lad," Blakely said with a glance at Lionel.

"You have to ride with us, Papa!" Jeremy shouted, bouncing a little in his vehemence. Lionel didn't even bother to hide his smirk.

Lady Blakely herself came to her husband's side and attempted to pry the child away. Jeremy clung to his father's neck like a monkey.

"You ride with us!" he said. His voice ended in a heartbreaking little sob.

"I'm so sorry," Vanessa said apologetically. "But the boys are accustomed to having you riding in the carriage with us, and Jemmy—"

"Yes, yes. I know," Blakely said with a sigh.

He gave Lionel a sheepish glance, confirming that his enthusiasm for a ride on horseback on such a cold day merely had been an excuse to isolate Lionel from the women.

"Not today, Jeremy," Blakely said again. The child's lower lip trembled threateningly. "Here, my lad," he added quickly to forestall the impending storm of tears. "How would you like to ride with *me* instead?"

Jeremy was instantly all smiles again, and a commanding look from Blakely's eyes silenced his wife's immediate protest.

"I suppose it will be all right for a quarter of an hour," she said hesitantly as she pulled the child's scarf up more firmly over his mouth and ears that barely protruded from a thick woolen cap. "He is bundled up warmly enough.

I am afraid that when Jamie sees him riding, he will fuss until he has his turn as well."

"There's a good fellow," Blakely said to his son, who promptly pulled the scarf down so it rested on his chin. Blakely nodded at his wife to show that he agreed to her conditions. Satisfied, Vanessa went to rejoin the search for the missing toy.

"I suppose, since you are so conversant with the details of my personal life," Lionel said glumly, "that Miss Whittaker has been apprised of all the sordid details of my disreputable past."

Blakely compressed his lips.

"I had to tell her *something* after the ball when she came to me with her precious scheme of inviting you to spend Christmas with the family," he said defensively as he put his delighted son in his saddle and held him in place as they walked. "I *thought* I had convinced her to see reason until I entered my drawing room yesterday and found *you* quite at home in it!"

Lionel shook his head in disbelief.

How like Blakely, in the guise of protective guardian, to rake up *that* old scandal to prove to Mary Ann just how little Lionel deserved her gratitude. Lionel marveled that Blakely couldn't have anticipated the outcome. Did he know his sister-in-law at all?

Mary Ann would never abandon her long-lost benefactor simply because he had brought the censure of the world down upon his head.

Oh, no. Not *she!*

Instead of despising him, as Blakely intended, the ever-helpful Mary Ann and her family naturally would be even more determined to repay their debt to a benefactor who had so clearly fallen upon hard times.

Apparently Lionel had been deluding himself that Blakely would think the tale unfit for her innocent ears.

It shamed him that the lovely innocent knew exactly why he was shunned by society.

Dash it! He longed to consign Blakely and his precious two thousand pounds to the devil and walk away with his dignity intact, but he couldn't do that to Garland. Lionel would survive the humiliation of being cast into the street for nonpayment of his rent, but the least he owed his faithful manservant was a roof over his head.

Lionel and Lord Blakely had been so intent upon their conversation that by the time they came back to the carriages from walking their horses, the missing toy had been found and order—such as it was in Lord Blakely's volatile household—had been magically restored. The servants had stopped to-ing and fro-ing from the coaches and had stepped back to stand at respectful attention in front of the house.

The gentlemen mounted their horses and prepared to begin the journey, only to find the whole enterprise halted again when young James, Blakely's firstborn, saw his brother sitting on the front of his father's saddle and threatened to throw another tantrum.

"Me!" he screamed from his perch in Mary Ann's arms. *"Me* ride with Papa!"

"Now, Jamie," Mary Ann said calmly, although she flinched a little at the boy's impassioned scream right in her ear. "What did Mama tell you about sharing? Jemmy will ride with Papa first. And then you may have your turn."

But Jamie was having none of it and his brother, fearful of being displaced, started fussing, too.

To Lionel's horror, Mary Ann calmly walked over to him and lifted the boy up.

"Look, Jamie," she said enthusiastically. "Mr. St. James's horse is bigger and faster than Papa's!"

"Miss Whittaker, what are you doing?" Lionel exclaimed, wide-eyed with alarm, as Blakely frowned at the aspersion on his horse's mettle. She was going to hand this wiggling scrap of humanity over to *him!* He knew *nothing* about children! What if he damaged it somehow?

As he had feared, she half-threw the boy into Lionel's arms, and he had no choice but to catch him. At a loss, Lionel awkwardly held the child out at arm's length and looked into his small, solemn dark eyes. He tried to give him back to Mary Ann, but she put her hands behind her back and playfully danced backward to prevent him from doing so.

"Blakely," he called out, certain of help from that quarter at least. Most devoted parents were quick to remove their impressionable children from Lionel's vicinity, presumably for fear his vices might somehow imprint themselves on their unformed minds. Lionel had not held a child in his arms for at least a decade, and he found it an alarming experience.

To Lionel's surprise, Blakely just looked relieved.

"Mind you hold him tight," Blakely said to Lionel. When Lionel hesitated, he added, "For God's sake *do* it, man, or we'll be lucky to be away by nightfall."

"If you wouldn't mind, Mr. St. James," Mary Ann said, smiling prettily at him, just as if he had a choice. Then she returned to the carriage, where her mother and sisters were waiting for her.

The still-dangling child looked up at Lionel with an expression of almost adult speculation on his face. Then, as if the stranger holding him had passed some obscure sort of inspection, Jamie smiled and reached his mittened hands out to Lionel, who interpreted this as a sign that he could lift him the rest of the way into his lap without risking a flood of terrified screams.

"Me ride," Jamie crowed happily. He gave his brother a superior smirk. "Bigger horse!"

He turned around to look at Lionel.

"Go fast," he said, grinning in a way that made Lionel give a surprised bark of laughter.

"Not *too* fast!" Lady Blakely shouted in alarm from where she was about to get into the coach with her mother and younger sisters.

Mary Ann gave Lionel a heart-stopping smile. Then she took her anxious sister's arm and gave her a gentle push into the traveling coach. She gave Lionel a coquettish little wave of farewell as the footman assisted her into the coach and closed the door with a snap.

All was in readiness at last, and the procession was off.

Lionel grasped the child carefully about his well-padded middle and set off at a sedate trot. When he passed the coach, Mary Ann's radiant face appeared in the window, and the smile she gave him was as warm as the small, wiggly bundle perched in front of him.

"Mr. St. James! I have been looking all over for you!" Mary Ann exclaimed when she found him in the stable with his horse. "What are you doing out here?"

He looked so dashing in his long dark riding coat that he took her breath away. He had rolled up the sleeves of his coat so that his strong wrists and forearms were bare, and a lock of lustrous fair hair drooped over his well-shaped brow. It was the first time they had been alone since that ruthless kiss he had forced on her, and she wondered if it was on his mind as constantly as it was on hers.

"I prefer to take care of my own horse," he said easily enough, but his eyes were cool chips of sea green glass.

Mary Ann did not understand. Alexander had issued orders for the care of all the animals upon arrival at the inn, and Mr. St. James must have known that his own horse, being in the party of so important a patron, would receive the stable's best attentions.

"But dinner is on the table," she persisted. "Alexander has procured a private parlor, and—"

"I am not hungry," he said. "Go in now, and leave me to my work."

She reached out and clutched his arm.

"Has Alexander said something to vex you?" she demanded.

The ice in his eyes thawed a little when he turned to face her.

"Nothing at all, my dear," he said mildly. "Go inside to your dinner."

"Do not be foolish. You must eat *something.*"

"Miss Whittaker," he said, giving her a look that made her draw her hand back at once, "I am neither a child nor an idiot. I will get something for myself when I am finished here."

"A greasy sandwich and a glass of local ale in the taproom, no doubt," she said with an indignant huff.

To her relief, he gave her a crooked smile.

"I happen to be quite accustomed to drinking local ale," he said. "And I have quite a fondness for greasy sandwiches."

"*We* have roasted chicken, a rack of lamb, a sirloin of beef, boiled potatoes, fresh-baked bread and mince pie," she said smugly.

"You do *not,*" he said, giving her a skeptical look.

But she grinned in triumph, because she knew she had him. There isn't a man alive who can resist a bloody hunk of sirloin and a slab of mince pie.

"Come and see," she said, nodding to a nearby groom to relieve Lionel of his brush. She took Lionel's arm and led him, unresisting, into the warm, bustling inn.

"You have become a prime favorite with Jamie," she said, enjoying the blush that crept up his lean cheek.

"Not I! It is Thunder to whom he has formed such a violent attachment," he assured her.

The boy, whose little face had been almost blue with cold by the time his fond Mama halted the procession and demanded that the boys be restored to the warmth of the carriage, had clung to Lionel and screamed with temper. Blakely had been forced to pry him loose.

Mary Ann smiled and was not fooled.

A kind and generous heart beat beneath Lionel's cool exterior.

If anyone deserved a Christmas miracle, it was he—and she prayed he wouldn't be *too* angry when he learned about the plan Vanessa already had set in motion.

"There you are, St. James!" Blakely said, sounding testy, when Lionel and Mary Ann entered the private parlor. "It's about time! We're *starving.*"

The table was positively groaning with food, and for a moment Lionel didn't understand. Then, when comprehension dawned on him, he was so surprised he just stood there, staring like a gapeseed.

They had waited for him. Just as if he mattered.

And he had deliberately lingered in the stable because he felt sure no one would be especially put out if he didn't join them. It never occurred to him that they would wait for him. It was almost as if he . . . belonged.

To his humiliation, a lump formed in his throat. He had not belonged anywhere in so long.

He didn't need this.

He didn't *trust* it.

That was another reason why he deliberately had set himself apart from them and lingered in the stable instead of coming inside. He needed time to remind himself that for all the ladies' seeming warmth toward a man who had once done them a service, he was not one of them.

Once the holiday was over, he and Garland would return to his shabby rooms in London, and he would once again be a parasite prowling the night for well-blooded hosts. And these respectable people would pretend not to recognize him if they happened to encounter him on the street. It was, after all, the way of the world.

"Mr. St. James! Sit by me!" said Aggie, making a place for him between herself and Jamie.

"Line-all!" shouted Jamie, reaching for Lionel with a big smile on his face. He bounced on the chair in his excitement.

Lionel told himself that the boy's enthusiasm was for Thunder and not for him, but he was still absurdly flattered.

"The food is not going to get any warmer, young man," Mrs. Whittaker reminded Lionel with a twinkle in her eyes, and everyone laughed merrily. It was a cozy little group. To Lionel's surprise, no servants waited at table. And there was not a nursemaid in sight. Lord and Lady Blakely were those rarest of all parents—those who actually *enjoyed* the company of their children.

And, heaven help him, he had enjoyed holding the boy on his lap and tucking him inside the skirts of his riding coat as they proceeded along the road, watching the crowded public coaches pass by with their horses' bridles decorated with red satin rosettes and the carcasses of Christmas geese and hams hanging from the doors and windows.

"Your pardon," Lionel said, remembering his manners as he accepted the offered seat with a smile for Aggie. "You did not have to wait for me."

"Of course we would wait for you. You are our guest," Lady Blakely said, surprised.

Temporarily, Lionel reminded himself firmly.

Lionel gave a mental shrug of capitulation. He wasn't really one of them, but he could enjoy the illusion while it lasted.

The clever Jamie crawled into Lionel's lap and, from

this higher vantage point, was able to snatch a piece of bread from Amy's plate.

Alarmed, Lionel caught the boy's hand.

"Is he old enough to eat that?" he asked, appealing to Lady Blakely. "He won't choke on it, will he?"

"Not if you break it into small pieces for him. He has a full set of teeth, I assure you, Mr. St. James," she said, smiling fondly upon him from her place at the foot of the table, where she was helping Jeremy eat. "But he cannot be permitted to eat bread alone, much as he likes it. If you would be so kind, cut a piece of your meat into little pieces for him and pour some gravy over it. And Jamie is fond of a few potatoes."

"You want *me* to feed him?" Lionel said, taken aback as he obediently tore off a small piece of the bread and permitted Jamie to stuff it in his mouth. Lionel anxiously watched the boy chew, poised to intervene at the first sign of distress. "Are you certain?"

"Well, Aggie can help him, if you would rather not, but Jamie has chosen you, and he is not likely to accept a substitute without a fuss."

How odd this seemed to Lionel. Most adults of his acquaintance had the children removed or punished if they dared to make a fuss at table. He had to admit, though, that the children were delightful company. To his surprise, the adults made no attempt to rush the children through the bountiful meal. When he commented on this, Lady Blakely informed him that when he married he would learn that children get cranky if they have to travel too long without a good long rest between stages.

When he married.

Not bloody likely!

"Jamie!" barked Lord Blakely when the little boy, intent on stuffing more food into his already full mouth, allowed a half-chewed piece of meat to dribble down his chin and onto Lionel's coat. Aggie captured the unappetizing bit in a napkin and set it aside. "Apologies, St. James. Our boy is a bit of a snatch-pastry."

"No matter," Lionel said when Lady Blakely gave an apologetic little cry of distress. "There have been worse things on it."

Much worse.

With a sigh of contentment, Lionel tucked into the meal, feeding little bits to Jamie, and enjoyed the cheerful chatter all around him.

When they reluctantly left the table and Lionel went outside with Blakely to mount their now-rested horses, he found Aggie at his stirrup.

"My turn," she said, grinning, as she held up her arms to him. Amy, he saw, was already perched on horseback with Blakely.

Lionel grinned back and hoisted her up so she could sit behind him and grasp his waist.

This isn't real, he told himself firmly. *It won't last.*

But, God help him, it felt good.

Six

Lionel and Lord Blakely rode on horseback the rest of the way to Leicestershire, an exercise that taxed both men's athletic ability to the limit.

In theory, either of them could have sought warmth and rest in the coach with Lord Blakely's family at any time, but Lord Blakely knew from sad experience that there was no rest to be found in a coach filled to the roof with high-spirited boys and their officious young aunts, and Lionel, because of the nocturnal nature of his profession, had far too few opportunities for a vigorous cross-country gallop.

He had been a bruising rider in his youth, and he found his body remembered the exhilaration of the exercise.

"Stop doing that," Blakely snarled. His breath streamed out in white puffs on the cold wind.

"What am I doing?" Lionel asked, surprised.

"Appearing to spectacular advantage on horseback, as if you didn't know. I feel sure the ladies are properly impressed, so you may safely relax into a canter and permit poor old Midnight to catch his breath."

Incredibly, there was a suspicious hint of humor in the viscount's voice. Lionel was happy to see that his once-convivial companion had not vanished entirely into the morass of patriarchal responsibility.

"I'd be happy to oblige you," Lionel answered with a rueful smile, "but it's the horse, you see. Thunder can't help but prance a bit in the presence of ladies. He's rather fond of feminine admiration, and I can't seem to break him of the bothersome habit."

Blakely gave a snort of amusement.

"I wish I didn't like you," he said grudgingly. "It would make you easier to despise."

"The feeling is entirely mutual, my lord," Lionel said, obligingly slowing his horse to a walk. "And you may despise me with my good will. It makes no difference to me."

Blakely gave a long sigh of remorse.

"You are not a bad sort, St. James," he said grudgingly. "You've won over my wife, my children, and I wish it could be otherwise, but—"

"You would rather see me roast in hell than have anything more to do with them," Lionel finished his sentence cheerfully. "It is quite unnecessary for you to belabor the point."

"The fair Barbara married her marquess and is now considered perfectly respectable," Blakely said a little too casually.

Lionel's jaw hardened.

"I have often heard it is a sign of impending senility when one suddenly starts rehashing scandals that are long out of date," Lionel said with a creditable assumption of kindly concern. "You want to keep up, old man."

"They are, by all accounts, wretchedly unhappy," the viscount persisted. "Her two youngest, it is said, were fathered by someone other than her husband."

Lionel raised one eyebrow.

"Well, don't look at *me!* I haven't been near the little hussy in ten years," Lionel said, rolling his eyes. "Is there some particular reason why you suddenly feel compelled to revisit this exceptionally painful episode in my dissolute past?"

"The young lady you abducted was fortunate," Blakely

said doggedly. Lionel gave him credit for the fact that he obviously was not enjoying this. "Her fiancé was willing to marry her anyway, and her family rallied around her. Another young lady—one not quite so happily situated— would have been utterly ruined. Mary Ann is like a daughter to me. In good conscience, I must take steps to protect her—"

"By ensuring that I don't misinterpret your forbearance and your family's friendliness as a sign that you would welcome me into the family," Lionel said stonily.

"Correct," Blakely said, looking uncomfortable. "For all I know, you may be a changed man. But I cannot take the chance—"

"Your precious sister-in-law is quite safe from me," Lionel snapped as he abruptly rode on ahead of his host to put an end to the conversation.

To the relief of all the travelers, the coach containing the family arrived at Lord Blakely's country house that same evening, albeit at an advanced hour. Blakely scooped up both his sleeping sons and carried them to the nursery with his wife, her two younger sisters and a gaggle of nursemaids trailing wearily behind him.

The gentlemen's valets and the ladies' maids had arrived slightly earlier, and Lionel found his necessities for the night carefully laid out in the comfortable chamber that had been assigned to his use. He waved his sleepy manservant away and ordered him to bed when Garland would have assisted him out of his clothes.

Even though every bone in his body seemed jarred loose from its socket and Lionel suspected that tomorrow he would not be able to move for creaking after the unaccustomed exercise of a day spent on horseback, his restless emotions would not permit him to sleep.

At home in London he would just now be embarking

upon his night's work at the tables, for the rich, fashionable gentlemen who were Lionel's prime targets often did not deign to appear in the gambling hells that featured the deepest play until after the evening's most exclusive *ton* parties were over and the ladies they escorted to these decorous affairs were safely confined at home.

Lionel disdained the easy pickings of the more accessible pocket-flush youths fresh from the country who were eager to squander their meager savings. To call Lionel a Captain Sharp was to do him an injustice. He never stooped to dishonest play with gullible opponents.

Where was the challenge in *that?*

Still dressed in his traveling clothes, he left the bedroom. A sleepy servant directed him to his lordship's library and built a fire there. Lionel then proceeded to sit in solitary state, smoking one of his host's excellent cigars and sipping on a glass of fine brandy. It was pleasant to be alone in such rich surroundings. Although the furnishings in some of the gentlemen's clubs he frequented were quite as impressive, there was no peace to be found there. Lionel decided to get drunk. This was a luxury an astute gamester rarely permitted himself because his fortunes depended upon the sharpness of his wits.

Another bit of self-indulgence he rarely permitted himself was the reflection that if his life had not gone so impossibly awry, by now he might be living in a house like this and have a brood of delightful children. Exhausting as he found young Jamie and Jeremy, the thought was unbearably sweet.

And maybe, if he were still the favored son and heir of Sir Andrew St. James, he might have met Mary Ann Whittaker again under different circumstances, and . . .

Lionel's hands tightened on the stem of his glass. With a sudden movement, he swallowed the contents in one gulp and welcomed the fire that burned in his throat.

He would *not* let himself think about that. He might be

a fool, but he drew the line at being a masochist. He re-filled his glass from the decanter and swirled it, admiring the rich, russet hue of the liquid.

Mary Ann Whittaker was not for him. All this was an illusion, a respite from his sorry existence. If the family's warm reception at dinner had misled him into thinking otherwise, Lord Blakely put an end to that notion soon enough.

Suddenly, a burst of coughing emitted from one of the darkened corners of the room, and Lionel shot to his feet. The smoke from his cigar had obviously flushed out a hidden observer.

"Ah, a spy," he said grandly as he peered into the shadows. "Come forth, spy, and join me in a glass."

He blinked in disbelief when the object of his reluctant longing stepped into the light.

"I couldn't sleep," Mary Ann said brightly as she waved her hand in front of her face to dispel the cigar smoke. "Why *will* men smoke those disgusting things? I thought I would see if I could find anything interesting to read."

There was something a little too gay in her voice. The girl was a shockingly inept liar, which set her apart from most of the women he had known.

"At this hour?" he asked skeptically.

She let her breath out in a sudden whoosh.

"All right, I followed you," she admitted.

"How . . . gratifying," he said carefully.

"Do you have everything you need?"

With a regretful sigh, Lionel stubbed out his cigar. A gentleman did not smoke in the presence of a lady, unless, of course she *was* no lady. Mary Ann Whittaker, despite her eccentric habit of stalking gentlemen unrelated to her in the middle of the night, was very much a lady.

"I am quite comfortable, I thank you," he replied with more courtesy than truth. Mary Ann had changed into a warm-looking gown of rich russet wool that added mysterious depths to her dark eyes. Her lovely hair was loose and flowing down her back, and he longed to lose himself in the silken strands. Comfortable? Hardly! He badly wanted to take her in his arms and find out if her lips were as sweet as he remembered.

She was difficult enough to resist in the full light of day when he was stone cold sober. Now, with fatigue and Lord Blakely's excellent brandy to weaken his defenses, he didn't know how he was going to keep his hands off her.

"You should not be here," he said when she approached and stood so close his senses were awash in her apple blossom scent.

"And neither should I, for that matter," he added with a deprecating gesture toward the now half-empty crystal decanter.

Mary Ann glanced at the decanter and then up at his face. She took her lush lower lip between her small white teeth for an instant, and he could see a pulse beat in the hollow of her throat, almost as if she feared him.

Well, she had bloody good reason to fear him!

Here she was, alone in the middle of the night with a man whose reputation was as black as his soul. A man with whom, by all accounts, no tender young virgin was safe.

"Well, that is all I wished to know," she said lamely. Her voice shook a little. "That you are comfortable, I mean."

"Good night, Miss Whittaker," he said pointedly.

Still she hesitated.

It seemed as if she would say something more, but she obviously thought better of it.

"I'll just go, then," she said reluctantly after a moment; then she turned toward the door.

"Miss Whittaker," Lionel said.

"Yes," she said, turning to him with a look of distress on her face.

"There is something else, is there not?" he asked quietly.

Mary Ann hung her head. When she spoke, her voice was barely audible.

"Vanessa invited your father to the party," she said.

It was the last thing he expected, and for a moment he just stared at her.

Then a loud, fervent exclamation that was definitely not fit for a young lady's tender ears burst from his lips. Mary Ann flinched, as if at a pistol shot.

"It was not her fault," she said, standing up to him. "It was . . . my idea."

"*Your* idea," Lionel repeated in a soft, dangerous tone of voice that made her flinch again.

"Yes. My idea." She bent her head so that the expression on her face was hidden by the lustrous curtain of her hair, but her shoulders trembled. "Alexander told me about . . . what happened between you and your father. He told me you were supposed to have abducted some woman."

"*Supposed* to have abducted?" Lionel repeated harshly. "Do you think me too noble to stoop to such perfidy?"

"Yes," she said defiantly. "I do. Alexander told me you were cast out by your family, and being your friend could only damage my reputation."

"He was right." Lionel wanted another drink. Very badly.

"But I thought if you could be reconciled with your father—"

"Then I would be a fit person for you to know," he finished for her. He shook his head in disbelief.

"Mr. St. James. *Lionel*," she said earnestly. "I do not care what Alexander says you have done in the past. I only know that you are a good person, and you deserve another chance."

"And *you,* in your infinite wisdom, have decided to give me one," he said angrily. "What gives *you* the right to meddle in my life?"

Mary Ann gasped when his fist hit the solid wall. His knuckles were probably bruised and might be bleeding, but he didn't care. The pain almost felt good.

"Confound it! They are supposed to be in Italy," he said. "They *always* spend the winter in Italy."

"They returned unexpectedly the day after the ball, and Melissa sent me a note. I bade Vanessa send them an invitation to the house party straightaway."

She couldn't quite look Lionel in the face.

Lionel clenched his fists and turned away from her to stalk to the fireplace and stare into the flames.

How like a woman.

Instead of despising him, as Blakely intended when he rehashed his sordid history for her edification, the ever-helpful Mary Ann would naturally decide that a Christmas party is just the setting for father and son to enact a tearful reunion.

That would tie up the problem of reforming Lionel's dissolute life with a big, fat, red Christmas bow, wouldn't it?

"Women," Lionel said aloud.

"I'm sorry," she said.

The sheer inadequacy of this statement surprised a snort of humorless laughter from him.

"Does *he* know *I* will be there?"

"No." She was squirming now. "Vanessa was afraid he might not come. She thought it would be best if you did not know, either, until it was too late for you to avoid the meeting. But I thought you might be even angrier if I did not warn you."

"Thank you for *that,* at least!" he said sarcastically.

"I'm sorry," she managed to force out.

"So you've said," he said in a carefully controlled voice that revealed how close he was to losing his temper.

"You must believe me." Mary Ann's eyes filled with tears.

"I believe you," he said between gritted teeth. "Your good intentions—misguided as they might be—were never in question. Now if you will excuse me, Miss Whittaker—"

"No, I will *not* excuse you! I was only trying to help. Why will you not forgive me?"

His control snapped; he seized her shoulders in his hands and half lifted her off the floor.

Mary Ann felt a thrill of danger at the unleashed strength of Lionel's arms and the compelling heat of his gaze. The amber lights in his green eyes made him resemble something dangerous, like a tiger at full attack. A nerve jumped at the junction between his cheek and jaw, and she could feel his hot, brandy-scented breath on her face.

"Because," he said in a low, husky voice, "I have not seen my father in ten years. Because I'm—"

"Afraid?" she suggested, and regretted her choice of words at once.

For a moment she felt his fingers tighten on her. Then he released her and let out all his pent-up breath in a rush.

"You don't know anything about it," he said when she rubbed her arms to dispel the numbness in them. She gave him a reproachful look, which he acknowledged with a shamefaced grimace. "I had no right to touch you like that. I beg your pardon."

"If you have left bruises on my arms, I am going to give you *such* a slap," she cried. To her humiliation, she felt a tear slip down her cheek.

"My father died when I was twelve," she said. "He was . . . difficult, to put it mildly. He didn't give my poor mother a moment's relief from anxiety. But a day never passes that I don't think about him and wish he had not died before I could tell him how much I loved him. Maybe it would have made a difference. Maybe he wouldn't have drunk so much. Maybe he would be alive today as a result. *Your* father is still alive. You can still make your peace with him."

Lionel touched her cheek and captured the tear with the pad of his thumb. The delicacy of this caress was such a contrast to his earlier roughness that the last of her defenses crumbled.

"It will not do, Miss Whittaker," he told her. "My father never admits a fault. He is a stubborn, selfish, egotistical man."

"So was mine," she said softly, "but he was still my father."

"He will never change."

"Mine might have. I'll never know now." The wistful sentence ended on a sob, and somehow Mary Ann was in his arms, pressing her face against the breast of his coat as he held her close. She could feel the warmth of his lips on her hair. He smelled of some spicy fragrance mixed with the scent of horse and the pure winter wind. It brought fresh tears to her eyes.

"Miss Whittaker," Lionel said reproachfully, rearranging her slightly so he could withdraw his handkerchief from a pocket and offer it to her. But her tears would not stop, so he tilted up her chin and gently wiped her eyes himself. "I apologized for manhandling you. What else do you want of me?"

"Speak to your father," she said brokenly, "before it is too late."

"Do not distress yourself." His voice was harsh again. "You were a child when your father died, so it is natural for you to grieve. But I am a grown man, too old to need a father, I assure you."

"You are wrong," she said, taking the handkerchief and turning away from him to blow her nose. "So wrong. I only wanted to—"

"I know what you wanted to do," he said with a wry grimace. "You wanted to repay me for the careless act of benevolence I perpetrated upon you all those years ago in a rash fit of generosity. You owe me *nothing,* Miss Whittaker. *Please!*" He closed his eyes as if in prayer. *"Don't* try to help me."

"But I—"

An angry voice barked out from the doorway, startling them both.

"What is the meaning of this?" Alexander demanded as he looked from Mary Ann's tear-blotched face to Lionel's implacable one with narrowed eyes.

"I . . . I . . ." Mary Ann looked to Lionel for guidance, but his sardonic expression was not helpful. She derived inspiration from his handkerchief, which was still clutched in his hand. "I had something in my eye," she said, sounding a little too happy about it. "I had something in my eye, and Mr. St. James removed it with his handkerchief."

It wasn't entirely a lie, she told herself. She *did* have something in her eye—entirely too many tears.

Alexander took a threatening step toward him, and Lionel turned, squaring his body to meet whatever retribution the viscount had in mind.

Mary Ann quickly placed herself between the two men.

"I came here . . . for something to read," she said.

"Did you?" Alexander said, clearly skeptical. "And what did *you* come here for, St. James?"

"A glass of your excellent brandy, of course," he said mockingly. "And a bit of privacy," he added pointedly.

"We'll leave you to it, then. Mary Ann," Alexander said with one imperative, uplifted brow as he crooked his arm to offer his escort. He apparently was taking no chances that she and Lionel would resume their tête-à-tête.

She accepted Alexander's arm and looked back at Lionel, who rolled his eyes with a comical grimace behind Alexander's stiff back and surprised an embarrassing spurt of laughter from her that she hastily turned into a cough.

What a man he is, she thought. One minute he made her cry; the next he made her laugh.

Whatever swing of emotion he provoked in her at any given moment, Mary Ann felt truly alive for the first time in her heretofore unremarkable existence. It was as if she had been waiting for him all her life.

Alone again, Lionel crossed his arms on the desk and rested his head against them. He didn't know whether to laugh or cry.

He did neither.

Instead, he poured himself another brandy and proceeded to get quietly drunk.

Seven

Lionel was lost in a delectable dream of Mary Ann Whittaker showering his face with ardent little kisses.

When he couldn't stand the delicious torture any longer, he took her hairy snout in his hand and trembled when her long, wet tongue swept enthusiastically along the entire length of his palm, leaving a juicy residue behind.

Hairy snout?

Long, wet tongue?

Lionel's eyes flew open. Then he shut them again. Tightly.

There was a big, hairy dog in his bed, and two giggling, dark-haired youngsters were peering at him from its foot.

Hoping he was dreaming but accepting the fact that it was highly unlikely, he cautiously opened one eye. The dog was leaning on all fours above him, anointing Lionel with its lolling tongue and warm, moist, pungent breath.

Just what he needed when all of the devils in hell were sitting on the bridge of his nose, gleefully having at him with a million tiny hammers.

He tried to push the dog down and found his fingers entangled in the dark, copper-hued fur instead. He couldn't resist stroking the hulking creature's back.

Lionel had been fond of dogs as a child, and he would have one yet if he had his way. Sometimes he got a bit lonely and longed for an affectionate, non-judgmental companion, but keeping a dog cooped up in his lodgings—especially a big one like the canine companions he remembered so fondly from childhood—would be unfair to the dog as well as to Garland.

He reflected that the relegation of an animal that would have made a superb hunting dog to his lordship's nursery for the amusement of a pair of mischievous children was just another example of how marriage had changed Lord Blakely.

Let this be a warning to a certain lonely bachelor who found himself captivated by a pair of warm, mischievous, chocolate-brown eyes and a mouth as rosy and sensual as a ripe strawberry.

Mary Ann Whittaker was not for him. In his mind he wrote it out and underlined it.

Wincing, Lionel forced himself to a sitting position and prepared to order the children out of his room.

He would have done it, too, and in no uncertain terms, if their big brown eyes didn't sparkle so much with expectant pleasure at him. His reluctant smile apparently encouraged them to grin and move in closer.

"We have been waiting for you to wake up," one of the boys said. This must be Jeremy, he conjectured, because the younger twin seemed to have a firmer grasp of the rules governing English grammar than his brother.

"Play with us!" commanded the elder as he jumped up on the bed and tugged on Lionel's sleeve. Lionel winced at the rocking motion of the bed. This would be Jamie. His speech seemed to consist entirely of commands and loud declarative sentences.

"Is Thunder awake?" Jeremy asked hopefully, clearly showing where his real affections lay.

The confounded little fellows were so appealing. In spite of his suffering, Lionel had to laugh out loud. He was punished almost immediately for this rash action when his head demons increased their hammering to a level just short of excruciating pain.

"Jamie! Jemmy! Go away *at once*," a feminine voice commanded in a mercifully soft—but no less firm—tone.

Mary Ann strode into the room with a tray containing a steaming beverage. Garland was right on her heels. Lionel frowned at his faithful manservant. Where had *he* been, Lionel wanted to know, when the boisterous twins invaded his bedchamber? He could not believe they had done so with any real stealth—not with a canine that weighed no less than seven stone in tow.

"Get up!" Jamie shouted cheerfully. "Put on clothes! Play with us!"

"Go," Mary Ann said to the boys. *"Now,* if you please! You, too, Whiskers," she added to the dog. It leapt from the bed, which caused Lionel's world to sway again. The boys ran away, giggling, and the dog raced after them, barking excitedly.

Lionel clutched his head to keep it from shattering into a thousand pieces.

"Miss, you must not disturb my master at this hour," Garland pleaded as he shot Lionel an apologetic glance.

"Nonsense. It is nearly noon," she said briskly. "And Mr. St. James will feel much more the thing when he drinks this."

Lionel pulled the covers to his throat with all the embarrassment of a timid virgin. He was covered in self-loathing at having her see him in his much-mended night shirt with his hair all on end and the unkempt stubble of a day-old beard on his jaw.

Mary Ann looked very fetching this morning in a warm wool day gown of celestial blue, and she brought the breath of spring and apple blossom scent into the room.

He reeked of night sweat and dog breath.

"Miss," Garland said, scandalized. "This is no place for you. If you will just give me the drink, I will—"

"No, Garland. He won't take it from you. He employs you." She had a bright, determined look on her face that struck terror in Lionel's heart. "Here, Mr. St. James. I've brought you something to make you feel better."

"What is it?" Lionel asked with great trepidation when Mary Ann gracefully sidestepped the agitated Garland and held the steaming mug to his lips. He looked down into the dark, purplish liquid and saw sinister yellowish clouds stirring in its depths. He had expected—prayed for—hot coffee or tea, but this was . . . something else. With great difficulty, he barely managed to refrain from casting up his accounts on Lady Blakely's daintily embroidered white linen sheets.

"It truly is better if you do not know," Mary Ann said gravely.

He put his hand over hers to keep her from tilting the repulsive brew into his mouth. It smelled worse than the dog's breath.

"It's perfectly harmless," she said soothingly, as if she were humoring a rebellious child. "It's my sister Lydia's special concoction. She used to make it for Papa when he was . . . not feeling quite the thing."

"Good God, girl!" Lionel said, offended. "I was not *that* drunk last night! I just have a bit of a head from—"

"So Papa always said, too," she said with a sigh. "Now, drink up."

"I assure you I do not make a habit of—" His words ended on a sputter when he was forced to swallow the liquid or allow it to spill down the front of him. He rather suspected it would make his skin smoke and turn his chest hair to brittle gray ash.

"Drink all of it," his fair tormentor said mercilessly when he would have turned his face away after a few sips. "If you stop for breath, you'll never get the rest of it down."

He was panting by the time he had drunk the horrid brew but, to his surprise, the nasty demons in his head magically took themselves and their little hammers off.

He sighed in blessed relief.

"There, now," she said, smiling encouragingly at him. Even so, there was disappointment in the depths of her lovely eyes. It made him feel ashamed. Deuce take it! "You'd better hurry if you want breakfast before the staff clears the chafing dishes away."

Breakfast.

The mere thought nauseated him, but he would rather die than let her believe he was so much the worse for drink that he couldn't drag his sorry carcass to the breakfast table like a civilized man.

"I am not a helpless drunk," he said defensively. It stung to have her look at him as if he were some broken derelict she had rescued from the gutter.

She bit her lip.

"Of course not," she said softly, and left him.

Mary Ann gave the tray and empty mug to one of the kitchen maids and scolded herself for her shock at the revelation that Lionel St. James—her knight in shining armor—was a drunkard.

Of course she had seen him drinking brandy last night. *All* gentlemen of any breeding drank spirits on occasion. But it never occurred to her that he, like her late father, might be a slave to this particular vice.

When Lionel had failed to come to breakfast, she looked in on him to find him groaning and tossing and turning as if in the throes of a nightmare. Alarmed, she had just determined he had no fever by touching his forehead when he rolled on his back and she got a whiff of the sour liquor on his breath.

She had feared he was ill from the long, cold journey from London on horseback, and she had come prepared to nurse him tenderly back to health.

Instead, she was appalled to discover that he was stinking drunk!

For a moment she had considered leaving him to suffer the effects of his self-destructive indulgence alone, but she found she could not do so no matter how much he deserved it.

He was an invited guest under her brother-in-law's roof. She was the one who invited him.

Not for the world would she have exposed her impressionable nephews to his disgraceful state. The little scamps must have escaped their nursemaids again and gone exploring. She could only hope they would not tell their mother about Lionel's drunkenness. She shuddered to think of Alexander's reaction to this latest evidence of her hero's iniquities. Fortunately, the boys were unaccustomed to such behavior and probably didn't understand what had occurred.

What had she expected? He was a professional gamester, for heaven's sake! Did she think he drank *lemonade* while he was on his night's raking plying his trade? For years she had demonized the faceless, nameless creature to whom her father had lost his fortune—a selfish, unscrupulous monster who callously exploited a discontented middle-aged man and left his wife and daughters to starve.

For the first time she realized that the monster could have had a handsome face. He could have been Lionel, or someone very like him, for all she knew. And the monster who ruined them, in turn, could have been an essentially good person led into bad habits.

Mary Ann's father had often insisted that he was not really a drunkard, just as Lionel St. James did. The late Mr. Whittaker had looked like he meant it, but he continued to drink, just the same.

She gave a sigh for the years she had spent romanticizing her knight in shining armor.

Her knight in shining armor. Hah!

She had wanted him to sweep her into his strong arms and carry her off on his white horse into a life of romance and adventure. Had she not waited for him *forever?*

But he was just a man, after all, as unique, wonderful and flawed as any other. Somehow, this kind and generous man had set himself on a crooked path to Perdition.

It was Mary Ann's duty to set him straight again.

Her father was dead, and it was too late to save him. Mary Ann would save Lionel, or die trying.

Eight

Lionel took extra pains with his appearance, as if to eradicate the signs of debauchery that had so dismayed Mary Ann. By the time he left his room, his pounding headache had abated to a dull thud by virtue of the concoction Mary Ann had forced him to drink.

Even so, he wasn't precisely grateful. Not even thorough rinsing with water seemed to remove the unpleasant taste from his mouth.

And he would never, as long as he lived, forget the disappointment in her eyes.

Never mind that he was *trying* to discourage her from thinking he was some schoolgirl's dream of a white knight.

Lionel had descended the staircase and was about to pass through the front hall on his way to breakfast when he came face-to-face with a very expensive blonde—for her fleeting affections had certainly proved expensive to *him*—in the midst of directing a small army of servants in the disposition of her luggage.

He stopped dead in his tracks and his jaw dropped. Lionel had spent a great deal of time during the past ten years mentally rehearsing what he would say to this woman if he ever saw her again, only to find himself speechless.

Upon spotting him, the lady's eyes went wide and she clutched her throat with one hand.

"You!" she gasped. She raised a languid hand to her brow and tottered as if on the point of swooning on her dainty, expensively shod feet.

Always the drama queen, was Barbara.

This bit of theatrics had the effect of loosening Lionel's tongue.

"None of that now, Lady Cavenish," Lionel said bracingly. "You've put on a good stone since I've seen you last, and I'm not feeling quite up to hefting you about. All these years of wicked dissipation are wearing on a man."

The lady gave Lionel a wounded look that should have melted his heart—if he had still possessed a heart.

In his assessment of her figure, Lionel did Lady Cavenish a grave injustice, and he knew it. She was and had always been a lovely woman, and if her figure was a bit fuller after the birth of three children, the result was not at all unattractive. Her provocatively cut traveling costume fit her like a second skin and was the color of ripe apricots. And if her pleated satin toque hadn't come straight from Paris, Lionel would eat it.

The lady's expression grew hard, effectively marring the impression of interesting frailty she had been at such pains to cultivate. She opened her mouth, presumably to annihilate Lionel for his ungallant observation, but Lord Blakely chose that moment to stroll into the hall.

"Ah, Blakely! Here's your man, Lady Cavenish," Lionel said cheerfully. "The fellow's as strong as an ox. Faint on *him*."

"Lady Cavenish. A pleasure," Lord Blakely said, kissing the hand she held out to him, wrist poised expectantly. His expression was surprised rather than pleased when he glanced at Lionel, and Lionel realized that the lady apparently was not on the official guest list. Interesting. He could acquit Blakely of this particular humiliation, at least.

"Good morning, Lord Blakely. How delightful to see you. I hope you do not consider this an imposition," she said, indicating the luggage with a pretty, fluttering gesture. "It is too naughty of me to come without an invitation, but I have just returned from the Continent, intending to surprise my sister with a Christmas visit, only to find that she and her family are promised to you and Lady Blakely for the holiday. I felt certain dear Lady Blakely would not mind if I came as well. It is *so* important for families to be together at Christmas, don't you agree?"

Lionel gave a snort of disbelief.

His father and stepmother were devilish high in the instep and considered Christmas one of those vulgar celebrations best left to the lower orders. It was never observed with any ceremony whatsoever in their home, nor, he would wager, in the equally snobbish Lady Cavenish's. The idea of these two worldly ladies falling into one another's arms in transports of Yuletide sentimentality was ludicrous.

Lady Cavenish favored Lionel with a frown of annoyance at his rude interruption.

"Your pardon, Lady Cavenish," he drawled. *"Pray* continue your tale."

She narrowed her eyes at him and turned again to her host.

"I would not inconvenience dear Lady Blakely for the world," she said sweetly to the viscount, "but then, little me can fit into any odd little corner that happens to be available."

"Such a pity there are no inns in Leicestershire," Lionel said pensively.

"Well, of course there are, silly boy," she said, batting him playfully on the arm. "I intended to find one, of course, as soon as I paid my respects to Lord and Lady Blakely, but Lady Blakely would not *hear* of my doing so!"

She finished this narrative with a blinding smile at Blakely.

Blakely.

Lionel narrowed his eyes and took a hard look at the his host, who blushed slightly and backed off from Lady Cavenish as if he feared he might be singed by the brilliance of that smile.

Of course.

Lionel was willing to wager his next large stake that Lady Cavenish had selected Blakely as a prospective partner for dalliance and, with characteristic audacity, she intended to beguile him right under his wife's unsuspecting nose.

Why else would she have come here uninvited?

He also was willing to bet that while the unsuspecting Lady Blakely had no idea the little harpy was after her husband, Lord Blakely himself was perfectly aware of it. Blakely's eyes were hard as he firmly detached the dainty beringed fingers that had reached out to grasp his arm.

"You knew, of course, my lord, that Lionel and I are related by marriage," she said sweetly. "Dear boy, you must tell me how you are getting on."

"Oh, I doubt that tale would be fit for your delicate ears, madam," Lionel said with equal sweetness.

At that moment, Lady Cavenish's maid entered the house with a large jewel case and a plump lapdog with ribbons artfully woven around its floppy ears. She was struggling to hold on to both cumbersome objects.

"*There* you are, you slow thing!" Lady Cavenish snapped, forgetting for a moment that she was a dainty, well-bred ornament of society whose normal speaking voice rarely rose above the merest whisper.

The maid cringed, but before her mistress could further scold her, Lady Blakely walked briskly into the hall with her housekeeper.

"Lady Cavenish. I'm sorry I was so long. A small crisis in the nursery," Lady Blakely said in pretty apology.

"All happily resolved now, I trust," Lady Cavenish said with a charming smile.

"Yes. Mrs. Simms will show you to your room when you are ready."

The housekeeper dipped in a curtsy.

"Thank you. I cannot tell you how much I appreciate your hospitality."

"It is our pleasure," Lady Blakely said, patting her hand. "We could not have you staying alone for Christmas, could we? I am sure I would have sent you an invitation if I had known you were in the country since, of course, you would want to celebrate the holiday with your sister. My own sister, Lydia, will not be with us this year, and I promise you that we will miss her very much."

"You *understand!*" Lady Cavenish said in a voice throbbing with emotion as she dabbed her perfectly dry eyes with a dainty square of lace-trimmed linen. "Is not Lady Blakely the kindest of hostesses, Lionel, and are we not most fortunate to find ourselves here?"

"Indeed," Lionel murmured.

Could it be that Blakely and the fair Barbara had already . . . transgressed?

If so, Blakely had a lot of nerve preaching propriety to *Lionel!*

Before he could speculate further, Mary Ann and her laughing younger sisters appeared in the doorway with their arms twined affectionately around one another.

"Ah, Lady Blakely! These must be your charming little sisters!" Lady Cavenish said sweetly. "What delightful children they are!"

Since she obviously included Mary Ann in this, the middle Whittaker daughter's usually warm brown eyes instantly turned to frost.

"Lady Cavenish, my sisters—Mary Ann, Amy and

Agatha," Lady Blakely said with an expectant nod at the girls. "My dears, Lady Cavenish has come to spend Christmas with her sister, Lady St. James, and with all of us, of course."

All three of the young ladies bowed.

Mary Ann regarded the stylishly dressed blonde with a gimlet stare. Her elder sister might be ignorant of the signs that a lady was on the hunt, but Mary Ann apparently was not. From the withering look Mary Ann gave Lionel, though, it was apparent that she considered *him* the lady's prey rather than Blakely. If Mary Ann had been a cat, her hair would be standing up all along her back.

She looked almost . . . jealous, and Lionel firmly repressed a foolish leap of his heart at this nonsensical notion. Well, Mary Ann had nothing to fear on that score.

The fair Barbara was every inch the sophisticated lady, but, at the risk of being ungallant once again, the bloom had been off *that* particular rose for some time as far as Lionel was concerned. Nor was she likely to look twice at him now that he had outlived his usefulness to her.

"You look familiar, my dear," she said at her most patronizing to Mary Ann. "Have we met? You surely must be out by now."

"Yes, I am out, my lady," Mary Ann said sweetly, "but I doubt if we move in the same circles. Your friends would be so much *older* than mine."

Lady Blakely gave her sister an incredulous look, and Lionel had to repress a nearly irresistible desire to applaud.

"Charming," Lady Cavenish said, showing all her teeth. "Well, I am quite fatigued after my journey." She cast a haughty glance at the housekeeper, who had been waiting patiently for the marchioness to notice her. "You, there," she said airily. "You may show me to my room now."

The housekeeper bobbed another curtsy and led the lady out.

At this juncture, Lionel longed to beat a strategic retreat in the firm belief that Providence had, at last, decided to punish him for every one of his sins.

Encountering Barbara, Lady Cavenish, with all her destructive arts and graces was *not* something that should happen to a fellow while his stomach was still queasy after a night of self-indulgence.

But when Lionel made for the door, he found it blocked by a determined Mary Ann.

"Are you in love with her?" Mary Ann demanded after she had taken his arm and practically dragged him into the hall.

To the point, as always.

"No," he said, appalled by the very thought.

A servant passed by, and Mary Ann caught Lionel by the wrist.

"We can't talk here," she said grimly as she towed him to a set of glass doors so frosted with moisture that at first he thought they opened to the outside. Upon closer examination, they proved to be the entrance to a lush conservatory.

Fascinated, he opened the door and allowed Mary Ann to precede him.

The air was filled with the scent of roses, lilies and other fragrant blooms. Classical statuary stood on pedestals along a stone mosaic path that meandered through the flora.

"What is this place?" he asked wonderingly.

"The conservatory?" She gave their lovely surroundings a dismissive glance. "Just another trifling token of Alexander's affection. Vanessa developed a passion for flower gardening when we were poor and quite beyond the pale, but getting dirt under her fingernails is hardly in keeping with her role as a viscountess and fashionable political hostess. Alexander had the conservatory built so she can dig to her heart's content whenever she is at leisure and have her own fresh flowers in the house the year around."

"It must have cost him a fortune," he said slowly. So lavish a gift might well betoken undying affection on the part of a devoted spouse—or a guilty conscience on the part of a philandering one.

"Well, yes. I believe it did," she said indifferently. "Never mind that. The harpy must want *you,* or she would not have bothered to force herself upon us."

Lionel blinked in confusion, then realized she had picked up the thread of her inquisition about Barbara. Mary Ann could give a terrier lessons on sheer, stubborn tenacity.

"*I* am not the one she wants," he said bitterly. "Women like her thrive on novelty and challenge, and I would be neither, I'm afraid. Not for the past ten years."

He watched her face in fascination as her intelligent brain grasped the riddle and solved it.

Her eyes opened wide and she gasped like a landed fish.

"You mean *she's* the one who—"

"I abducted?"

"The one whom you are *said* to have abducted."

Lionel had to laugh at that.

"Ah, my dear," he said, shaking his head with affectionate amusement. "You will not believe the worst of me, will you?"

"Never! Especially now that I have met her," she said with a sniff. "She must be thirty years old!"

"A trifle older than that, I fear," he said ruefully. "But then, I am just turned thirty myself."

"Well, she looks *much* older than you," she said

sheepishly, conscious that she had committed a faux pas. "It must be terribly painful for you to see her again. I would not have subjected you to this embarrassment for the world! She wants you back, of course. How perfectly dreadful for you!"

Lionel's heart melted. It had been a long time since anyone worried about *his* feelings.

He brushed her cheek with his knuckles.

"I assure you, the lady did not come all the way to Leicestershire in pursuit of *me*."

"No one dresses like that for a simple country house party. It is plain she is here in pursuit of *someone,* and it *isn't* her sister! If not you, who could it be?"

"I neither know nor care," he lied.

But he could see by Mary Ann's expression of horror that she had come to his own conclusion.

"She *wouldn't!"* she gasped. *"Alexander?"*

Lionel made an ironic pantomime of applause.

"But he is *married!"* she cried. "With *children!"*

"Mary Ann, Mary Ann," Lionel said in a pitying tone at her naïveté. "So is *she,* after all. An affair with a married man is irresistible to a lady who wants to indulge in a risk-free romantic encounter and continue to enjoy all the prerogatives that accompany her husband's rank. And if he is a devoted husband and father, the pleasure of conquest is all the keener."

She gave him a look of pure, unadulterated disgust.

"Do you expect me to believe that she is after Alexander, when *you* are here?"

"How vastly flattering!" he said dryly. "You forget that she did not know I had accompanied you to Leicestershire until she saw me this morning."

And a nasty shock it was, too, he was willing to wager.

"Odious woman! I wish she would go away."

"I *could* make the supreme sacrifice and abduct her again, I suppose," he suggested with a martyred sigh.

"Will you be serious?"

"All the gentleman has to say is 'no,' after all. Do you think he won't?"

Mary Ann's face was adorably transparent. Every emotion bloomed across her pretty face for all the world to see.

"Of course he will!" she insisted in a tone that suggested she was trying to persuade herself as much as Lionel of this.

She plopped down on one of the little stone benches in front of a white marble statue of Diana the Huntress.

What a lovely picture she made in her blue dress, framed against the yellow roses. He concentrated very hard on her words to keep from being distracted.

"That is, I would trust Alexander with my life, but women like *her*—" she was saying.

Lionel couldn't help taking her hand and kissing it.

"Blakely is in love with his wife. Any fool can see that, my dear. He is not about to risk losing her for a casual affair with the fair Barbara," Lionel said comfortingly. He hoped it was true. "I think you overestimate the lady's fatal charms."

"You are right, of course," Mary Ann said. She looked up at him with a grateful smile. "Thank you, Mr. St. James. You have made me feel so much better."

With that, she rose and waved at her beckoning younger sisters and her nephews, who were standing at the glass door, making faces at Mary Ann and Lionel, and drawing pictures in the fog on the panes.

"I promised to take my sisters ice skating, Mr. St. James," she said, looking over her shoulder at him. "Will you join us?"

"No, I thank you," Lionel said.

His mind conjured an enticing vision of Mary Ann gliding across a frozen pond in his arms, shrieking with laughter, but he had other fish to fry today.

Someone had to keep an eye on Barbara.

Nine

"Let's have a round tale from you, my lady," Lionel demanded once he managed to whisk Barbara into Lord Blakely's library. It had the advantage of a door that closed. "And spare me that nauseating drivel about wanting to spend Christmas with your affectionate sister."

The marchioness's eyes glittered.

"You know, I quite like this masterful side to you, Lionel."

She leaned forward, just a little, to give him a tantalizing glimpse of the round tops of her breasts in a neckline that was cut a bit lower than was precisely proper for daytime wear.

He wasn't even tempted to look.

"Cut line! What are you doing here, Barbara?" he demanded.

"Nothing that need concern you, darling," she said silkily as she ran a hand up his sleeve. He did not give her the satisfaction of responding in any way. "I did not ask what game brought *you* here to roost with these very plump pigeons. If your goal is to fleece Lord Blakely of his money or seduce his charming little wife, it's all the same to me."

Lionel stared at her for an incredulous moment. He had thought he was no longer capable of being hurt by anything this woman said to him, but he had been mistaken.

"These are good people, Barbara," he said reproachfully.

"Why, yes," she said. "So they are." She licked her lips provocatively. "Especially Lord Blakely. I expect he is very, very good, indeed."

"It *is* Blakely, then!" Lionel exclaimed. "I *knew* it."

The lady burst into a trill of laughter.

"Wouldn't *you* like to know!" she said mysteriously.

"Who else would it be?"

"Do you think I'd tell *you* my plans so you can spoil sport? Hardly! Isn't it providential that my sister was invited to Lady Blakely's party so I would have an excuse to come as well?"

"And how is your devoted husband?" Lionel asked dryly. "In good health, I hope. And your children. There are three of them, are there not?"

"Gentlemen's libraries are such practical things," she said, idly running her finger down the row of glittering crystal decanters filled with varying hues of liquor that shimmered like jewels in the light of the large bay window. "Ladies' salons are so ill-equipped by comparison."

Barbara helped herself to a glass of Lord Blakely's excellent brandy and drank it straight down. The decanter magically had been replenished after Lionel's own forays into it the night before.

Lionel reflected that for all her gaiety, Barbara didn't look happy.

"Ah, that's better," she said with a sigh.

"I say, Barbara," Lionel protested in astonishment. "You don't make a habit of *that* sort of thing, do you?"

She didn't even cough after she poured another glass and drank enough of the fiery liquor straight down to stagger a man.

"And why shouldn't I?" she said tightly, "My husband, to answer your question, is in Italy, nursing his gout and consoling himself with his latest paramour. My children, heaven be praised, are in the care of an excellent staff of devoted nursemaids at our primary seat and will miss me not at all."

She took a deep breath and fixed Lionel with a melting look from her large, slightly sunken blue-gray eyes. He once had thought Barbara's eyes dreamy and poetic. Had they always looked so predatory?

"I've been so *very* lonely, Lionel," she said soulfully as she laid an expensively gloved hand on his arm.

Lionel gave a snort of rude laughter and shook off her hand.

"Not *very,* if half the tales I hear of your amours are to be believed, my sweet," Lionel said with a wolfish grin. "Now, what do you want with Blakely? He's a stolid old married man. Not quite in your style, I should think."

"I have not *said* I am after Lord Blakely," she reminded him coyly. "But I *will* say I have an infallible instinct for these things, and I can sense the banked fire beneath his placid domesticity. Have you never heard him speak in Parliament?"

"I can't say that I have," he said, giving her a skeptical look. "Have *you?*"

"Oh, *yes,*" she sighed, holding one fluttering hand to her heart and rolling her eyes heavenward. "Such fire! Such *passion!* A man who can get so worked up over dreary old laws and taxes must be capable of an all-consuming love."

She gave a delicate little shiver of rapture.

"Well, no doubt you're a better judge of these things than I," Lionel said, unimpressed, "but from what I've seen, his only all-consuming romantic passion is for his very beautiful wife."

"What utter nonsense! He would have you believe he has not so much as *looked* at another woman since he married that little nobody, and I see you have been taken in by all the rest. Think of it, Lionel. All that *passion* simmering under the surface of that magnificent body, ready to be unleashed by—"

Lionel recoiled with a grimace.

"Barbara, I beg of you! Spare me *that* pretty picture." Her face softened.

"Poor Lionel. For what it's worth, I have regretted the decision I made that night ten years ago a thousand times," she said with a little catch in her voice. She sounded almost as if she meant it, but she always did have a flair for theatrics. "It is not a pleasant thing to break a man's heart."

Lionel hunched a shoulder and turned away from her.

"You flatter yourself, madam," he said curtly.

"Still bitter after all these years," she said with a sigh. "Well, I don't blame you, Lionel. Truly. But you were already ruined the moment they caught up with us. You were always *very* wild, and your father was *very* angry. He was sure to disinherit you anyway, with my sister fanning the flames. I ask you, what purpose would have been served by *my* ruination as well?"

"None at all," he agreed, oddly fascinated by the specious logic she used to justify the lie that resulted in his estrangement from his father.

"I was weak and frightened," she admitted. "I *am* sorry. If I had it to do over, I would defy them all and follow my heart. I have learned that life without love is truly meaningless, and my life has not been a happy one. Do try to pity me a little, darling."

"*Pity* you! You *dare* say that to me?" he said in disbelief. "Spare me the Cheltenham tragedy, madam. You made your choice to marry the marquess long ago. It is too late for repining now."

"But Lionel! You are wrong!" she said. "I have found love at last."

"If rumor is correct—and it is rather too persistent not

to be—you have found love, as you choose to call it, not once but many times since you married your marquess."

"Those affairs were to punish my philandering husband. This is different," she said, eyes shining. "I am going to leave Giles and start my life over again, fresh and new, somewhere on the Continent with *him*." She gave a little giggle of anticipation. "My love doesn't know yet. I have come all this way to tell him."

"Leave your husband after all these years? Are you *mad?*" cried Lionel.

"No. I have finally become sane!" she declared. "So, let us come to an understanding. I won't interfere in whatever game you're playing, and you won't interfere with me. Our goals are not mutually exclusive, you know. You can either make love to the little wife or take advantage of Blakely's inattention to win a great deal of his money from him. I care not which."

"You would destroy a perfectly healthy marriage for sport?" Lionel asked incredulously.

"Darling," she said, as if he were the most naive person in the world. "A 'perfectly healthy marriage'?" she scoffed. "There is no such thing, I assure you. And I should know."

Lionel raised one eyebrow.

"Who is bitter now?" he asked softly.

Barbara pursed her lips in annoyance and did an agitated turn about the room.

"You disappoint me, Lionel. I thought you and I, of all people, were above such bourgeois morality."

"My apologies," he said with a deprecating wave of his hand. "At the risk of lowering myself further in your esteem, I must confess the thought of accepting Lord Blakely's hospitality so that I may fleece him of his money or make free with his wife is utterly repugnant to me."

Lady Cavenish looked perplexed.

"If not the wife or his money, then, what—" Her eyes widened, and she gave him a look of utter disbelief.

"Not that great, cow-eyed girl!" she exclaimed, sounding perfectly revolted.

"As far above my touch as the wife, I'm afraid," Lionel said with a lightness he didn't feel.

"I say, what are you going to do when your father and my sister arrive? You *did* know they were expected?"

When Lionel remained silent, her eyes widened.

"Of course," she breathed, "you are going to try to reconcile with your father and cut Julian out! How positively *brilliant!* I would wager my last *sou* that he has no idea you're here, and when he gets here it will be too late."

Lionel gave her a sardonic bow. If she was determined to find an ulterior motive for his presence in Leicestershire, this probably would do the least harm.

"You must forgive me for misjudging you," she said with genuine remorse.

She *would* think better of him if she thought he meant to rob Julian of his status as heir!

"So don't interfere with me, Lionel," she continued, walking her fingers up the lapel of his coat, "or I shall tell all to dear sister Beatrice. I am afraid she will be quite put out, for she has *such* plans for this visit. She is determined to inveigle Lord Blakely and the Earl of Stoneham into taking up her dull little pet, Julian. The poor, deluded woman thinks her darling boy is cut out for a brilliant career in government, can you *imagine?"*

As she trespassed up his coat, she got closer and closer until she was a mere kiss away. Her perfume surrounded him in a sticky-sweet cloud.

"Actually, no," Lionel said, stepping back to avoid her lips. "I *can't* imagine because I haven't seen or talked to Julian for ten years, as you well know."

"Oh, yes," she said airily as the barb went sailing over

her head. "Suffice it to say that only connections in high places would serve to obtain any kind of distinction for a dull dog like *him*. No doubt it will give you *great* satisfaction to learn that your father is quite disappointed in him."

"This may surprise you, Barbara, but that gives me no satisfaction at all," Lionel said, clenching his jaw.

"Nonsense," she said. "Of course, Beatrice will expect me to upset the butter boat over Lord Blakely on Julian's behalf, but it would be more amusing to work on *your* behalf instead."

She lowered her voice to a throaty whisper as she advanced upon him.

"The gratification," she purred, "would be *so* much greater. Do let me help you. It is the least I can do to make amends."

"Perhaps when hell freezes over," he said, smiling in a way that showed all of his teeth.

"I suspect Lord Blakely is not the only one with hot passions smoldering beneath the surface," she crooned as she drew one finger across his jaw and leaned forward until she was practically in his arms. She reached up to embrace him, and Lionel realized that he had been mistaken in his impression that the lady was unaffected by all the liquor she had consumed.

Lionel very carefully removed her clutching hands from around his neck. Otherwise, the suppressed fury in him might have broken her wrists. Taking no offense, she merely laughed and danced away.

"I am in love for the first time since we parted ten years ago," she said soulfully. "*Do* try to be happy for me, Lionel."

Lionel gave a strangled groan of disgust and left the room to keep from throttling her.

How could he ever have thought himself in love with such a creature?

She must not be permitted to destroy Lord and Lady Blakely's family. Lionel would stop her with the last breath in his body.

In a regular lather of frustration, he summoned Garland to bring him his greatcoat and strode out into the beautiful winter day. The ground was blanketed with snow, but now the sky was an almost blindingly glorious blue with big, fluffy clouds dancing across it. The sun was shining. The air was crisp with promise.

So the sky of Eden must have appeared before the loss of innocence.

He went to the stable to check on his horse, a habit he had cultivated after years of boarding his cattle in commercial stables, even though he had no intention of riding. Unless one made a habit of dropping in unexpectedly, one could not be sure one's horse was receiving proper care.

On impulse, he changed his mind and decided a brisk ride was just the thing to clear his head, even though he would have recoiled in horror an hour ago at the thought of scrambling his brains inside his throbbing skull. He had wanted nothing so much upon awakening as to topple back into the comfortable bed and pull the linens over his head. Now his brain was seething with conjecture.

He waved away the groom who would have saddled Thunder for him and did the task himself. The earthy smell of hay and horse soothed him.

Lionel had been gone from the house for an hour and was on his way back to the stable when he came upon a small blue-coated figure walking along the curved path. He slowed to a walk to avoid startling the youngest Whittaker daughter and tipped his hat to her.

"Good afternoon, Miss Agatha," he said politely. Her eyes warmed with recognition, and Lionel couldn't help smiling. Few people looked at him with such honest, uncomplicated pleasure. He noticed that she carried a pair of ice skates in her hand.

"Good afternoon, Mr. St. James," she replied. "Will you give me a ride to the pond on your horse? I am in a great hurry because Mama says Mary Ann must return to the house to dress soon for afternoon calls, and Mary Ann will make us return with her as well because we are not allowed to be on the pond alone."

Lionel had intended to avoid Mary Ann until he had a chance to think through this new development with Barbara, but he could hardly rebuff a child who was smiling at him so expectantly. She held her arms up, and he swung her onto the horse, where she perched behind him and laughed out loud in girlish exuberance.

"You can see so much more from up here," she said, looking around with bright-eyed interest. "It must be a very great thing to be tall."

"Well, yes. It is, rather," he said on a startled chuckle.

Lionel had missed having children in his life, although no amount of torture could have compelled him to admit it. Aggie's small hands resting so trustingly on either side of his waist gave him a sharp, poignant memory of his little half sister in the years when he had been her devoted big brother. And Julian, as a stout, earnest youth, had been equally endearing in his own way.

Following Aggie's instructions, they soon arrived at the pond where Mary Ann and her other sister, Amy, were laughing and holding on to each other, lurching erratically. Aggie quickly donned her skates and glided onto the ice to join them.

Lionel had intended to return to the house immediately, but he could not resist stopping to watch.

When Mary Ann laughed, she laughed with her whole body. Not for her the restrained, ladylike titter of other females in society. He could hear her merry shrieks clearly from across the frozen surface. Her unaffected mirth made him smile, even though his head was troubled. She was warmly wrapped up in a burgundy pelisse trimmed in silver fur.

The girl seemed to have a different stylish, fur-trimmed coat for every day of the week. He imagined few royal princesses had such extensive wardrobes.

Both of her sisters struggled valiantly to keep Mary Ann upright, but they were losing ground because her infectious laughter had spread to them as well, and soon they were all wheezing for breath.

Suddenly they lost the battle, and Mary Ann fell to the ice, hard, on her bottom. Each of her sisters took one of her hands and tried to haul her to her feet.

Mary Ann's throat was raw because of the great gulps of cold air she was taking into it, but she couldn't help laughing all the harder because of her sisters' determined tugging and pulling.

It was just so ridiculous and so embarrassing. Her mother would be horrified if she could see her now, sitting on the ice with her legs and elbows all akimbo. Ladies did *not* laugh so hard that their bellies shook.

"It's no use," Amy said fatalistically. "She's too heavy."

"Mr. St. James!" said Aggie, looking beyond Mary Ann with a smile of appeal on her face to the man who apparently had approached the sisters unseen by Mary Ann. "Maybe you can bring your horse onto the pond and pull Mary Ann up with a rope, like Alexander did with the plow horse that laid down last spring and couldn't get up. Remember, Mary Ann?"

Mary Ann sobered instantly, mortified that Lionel St. James, of all people, had witnessed her undignified performance. And how like the well-meaning but tactless Aggie to call attention to Mary Ann's ungainliness by comparing her to a big, clumsy old plow horse in front of a gentleman. She didn't dare turn around to face him.

"I do not believe that will be necessary," his deep,

amused voice said from behind her. His strong hands went under Mary Ann's arms and hauled her effortlessly to her feet. When her skates started sliding from beneath her, he grabbed her about the waist and held her back against his chest to keep her from falling. "Steady, there."

Her ankles had never been particularly strong, which was one reason why she was such a clumsy skater. It didn't help that Lionel's arms around her made her weak at the knees.

"Mama says we must return to the house in half an hour," Aggie reported.

"Very well," Mary Ann replied, striving not to croak. It was hard to speak in a normal tone of voice when she could feel the warmth of Lionel's hard body all along her back.

Amy and Aggie skated around them once and glided off across the pond.

"They're charming girls," Lionel said.

"Yes," Mary Ann replied, self-conscious at standing on the ice with his arms still around her. She had to move away from him before she disgraced herself further. "You may let go of me now."

"Are you sure?" he asked skeptically.

He must think her a great, clumsy ox, Mary Ann thought resentfully.

"Certainly," she said. "Release me, if you please, Mr. St. James."

When he obeyed, she tried to skate a bit away from him to give herself distance and a modicum of dignity. Unfortunately, she set one skate awry in her nervousness and had to windmill her arms to keep upright, which wasn't easy within the confines of the narrow, fitted sleeves of her coat. Lionel caught her arms just above the elbows to keep her from toppling over on her backside again.

Mary Ann was embarrassed but grateful. She had no wish to bruise her tender anatomy further.

With great difficulty, she gained her feet and managed, with Lionel's help, to turn around so she could face him as she held on to him for support. She looked up into his eyes and her breath caught in her throat.

If he did not stop smiling at her like that, she was likely to overset them both.

"I think we had better make for land," he said, grinning.

"Yes," she replied wryly. "It will take the entire half an hour for me to get off the pond at this rate."

"Not necessarily," he said, and lifted her into his arms.

"You will strain yourself," she said. She could feel her face turning red. She never had been held in a man's arms before, and the sensation was quite as alarming as it was pleasurable.

He only smiled and started striding toward the shore. Mortified, Mary Ann could hear her sisters applauding and cheering behind them.

Ten

Mary Ann hadn't a bit of guile in her, which made her a refreshment to Lionel's soul after dealing with the duplicitous Lady Cavenish.

Lionel lowered Mary Ann as if she were made of spun glass onto the trunk of a fallen tree and removed her skates as she continued to blush a lovely shade of pink. She tried to convey the impression that gentlemen performed such personal services for her every day, but her lips trembled.

Such lush, tempting lips.

Her gloved hands fluttered as if she didn't quite know what to do with them before she finally clasped them in her lap.

For all her outward sophistication, Mary Ann wasn't accustomed to the touch of a man.

Lionel wished with all his heart that he was the prince destined to awaken this sweetly sleeping beauty.

But he wasn't.

He never would be.

"I can do it myself," she said. Her voice quavered endearingly.

"Allow me," Lionel insisted, reluctant to release her.

He was very much afraid that for the next week he would invent all sorts of excuses to have his greedy hands all over her.

Lionel gave Mary Ann's left boot a squeeze to indicate that it was free of the skate and he was ready for the other.

Her ankles looked delicate, even through the leather boot. Not a sufferer from false modesty, Lionel would have attributed her lack of coordination on skates to the proximity of a presentable-looking male to catch her in his arms if she had not exhibited her ineptness *before* she knew he was watching.

He almost commented on her uncharacteristic silence, but he forbore to tease her. He might not have been much in the petticoat line these past years, but he knew a woman in love when he saw one.

Instead, he completed his task and took her hands in his to help her arise from the fallen tree.

Mary Ann's breath caught as she looked up into his eyes. She was so very sweet when she wasn't engaged in turning his life upside down.

She disarmed him completely by clinging to his hands for a moment when he would have withdrawn them.

"I wish you could always be like this," she said with a tremulous smile, echoing his own thought.

No guile at all.

Before he could stop himself, he bent and kissed her lips.

Just a taste, he told himself, knowing he was playing with fire.

Mary Ann put her arms around his neck and kissed him back with all the ardor in her earnest young heart.

She was so sweet, so soft, so beautiful. Her ardent and not very expert kiss was a refreshment to his jaded senses. He wanted it to go on forever, but, if he truly cared about her, it must end *now*.

Reluctantly, he broke off the kiss and touched his forehead to hers.

"This was very different," she said.

"Hmmm?" He knew for the rest of his life he would associate bright winter sunlight with the scent of apple blossom.

"From when you kissed me before," she explained. Her eyes were shining.

"My good girl," he said in dismay. "Do not tell me— *please* do not tell me that was your first kiss."

Her bowed head gave him his answer.

"What a brute I am!" he said, appalled. "I am so very sorry. A first kiss should be . . . memorable."

"Oh, it was," she said ruefully.

She leaned forward and closed her eyes in unmistakable invitation; Lionel cast caution to the four winds and reached for her again.

Before he could commit any further exploration of Mary Ann's tender mouth, however, Amy and Aggie noisily scrambled onto the fallen log and waited expectantly for Lionel to remove *their* skates for them. Their eyes were twinkling. He had forgotten all about them in the pleasure of kissing Mary Ann.

Lionel was hardly a match for the girls' mischievous smiles, and he accomplished the task with much joking on his part and giggling on theirs. He remembered skating with his little half sister and half brother in happier days, and the hardened shell around his heart cracked a bit wider.

Thunder rolled an expressive eye in Lionel's direction at the indignity when he lifted the younger girls to sit in the horse's saddle and took the reins in his hand to guide the horse toward the house. He lightly grasped Mary Ann's elbow with his other hand, ostensibly to guide her over snowdrifts and other obstacles, but he really just wanted to touch her.

Lionel found his steps lagging.

His lungs expanded in the cool, crisp air and his eyes lifted to the blue vastness of the cloud-scattered sky as Aggie gleefully described the macaroons and other pastries she had seen Cook preparing for the delectation of Lady Blakely's guests and afternoon callers.

If Lionel had his way, he would make this walk to the house last forever. What more could a man ask than the company of his horse, two happy youngsters chattering animatedly without drawing a breath and a beguiling woman whose kisses made his heart leap in his breast?

Unfortunately, once they arrived at Lord Blakely's country house, Mary Ann would go to her room to change into proper young-lady-receiving-at-home attire, Amy and Aggie would go off to the nursery to herd their young nephews around like affectionate sheepdogs and he would have to deal with the devious Lady Barbara and the impending arrival of his estranged family.

This last unwelcome intrusion occurred sooner than he expected, for they neared the house to find a huge coach disgorging its passengers.

Lionel felt his face tighten with foreboding as he helped Aggie and Amy down from the horse's back and relinquished Thunder's reins to one of the attentive liveried servants who always seemed to be hovering about, waiting to perform a service for Lord Blakely's family and guests.

Lady St. James emerged from the coach and gave a hiss of displeasure at the sight of Lionel.

She just stood there in speechless indignation and might have brushed by him without speaking if Melissa hadn't followed her mother from the coach, gasped loudly and broken into a wide, affectionate smile at the sight of him.

"Lionel!" she cried, sounding a bit giddy. Tears sprang to her eyes and made them glitter like sapphires. "Is it really you?"

Lionel had to blink rapidly or risk disgracing himself. She was wearing a rose pink bonnet that was now slightly askew over her golden curls. He hadn't seen her since she was ten years old, but her face was still as round and sweet as the first wild rose in springtime for all that she was a young lady now, with three London seasons behind her.

Lady St. James gave a squeak of indignation when

Melissa flew into Lionel's arms. At first he stood stock still, as if his body was suddenly turned to wood. Then he returned Melissa's affectionate hug and kissed her temple. He held her by her shoulders and just looked at her.

"You've grown up, 'Lissa," he said, embarrassed by the huskiness in his voice. It touched him immeasurably that she not only recognized him but greeted him with such unreserved affection.

"Of course, you silly. I have missed you so much," she whispered, giving him another hug.

Then she spotted Mary Ann, gave another girlish squeal and enthusiastically hugged her friend as well.

"Mary Ann! This is the most *wonderful* surprise! Lionel is my brother, did you know?"

"Yes," Mary Ann said, obviously thrilled with Melissa's reaction to the "surprise."

"Melissa!" snapped her mother in a tone of voice that cracked like a whip.

The young lady was saved from the furious scold that no doubt would have followed by the arrival of Sir Andrew St. James and his heir, Julian, on horseback. Melissa might have blossomed in the years of Lionel's estrangement from the family, but one could hardly say the same for Julian. He had been such an open, pleasant, good-natured podge of a boy. He had made quite a pest of himself, following Lionel around like a devoted puppy.

Julian was still a portly fellow, but now his face was set in a peevish expression. He had a pained look about his mouth that gave Lionel the impression that his shoes pinched.

But the greatest shock was his father.

Sir Andrew was still recognizable as the vigorous country gentleman Lionel had always known and once believed as omnipotent as one of the sterner dwellers of Mt. Olympus, but now his hair was nearly all gray, and there were unfamiliar lines in his once-handsome face.

He looked . . . old.

Well, living with his darling Beatrice would age any man, Lionel thought wryly.

She had turned purple, as if she were about to suffer an apoplexy.

Lionel could only hope.

"We will leave at once," Sir Andrew gritted out through clenched jaws.

His wife gave a smug sneer in Lionel's direction and motioned for her daughter to precede her into the carriage, but Melissa cried out in distress and took a stand next to Lionel. Her small, cold hand grasped his tightly, as if she was afraid her mother might tear her away from him.

"Go if you must, but *I* am staying!" she declared. Her eyes flashed defiance. Melissa might *look* like the first rose of summer, but Lionel recalled that she could be as obstinate as a mule when she chose, bless her. It was evident that she and her bosom bow, Mary Ann Whittaker, had much in common.

"Of course you must stay," Mary Ann said soothingly. "Please, Lady St. James, Sir Andrew. Do not go, I beg of you. It's *Christmas.*"

Lionel watched with sardonic amusement while Lady St. James weighed her dilemma. He knew that while she was perfectly capable of giving her stepson the cut direct and humiliating a rebellious daughter with a few razor-sharp words, his socially ambitious stepmother would not want to show this ruthless side of her character to a relative by marriage of the viscount who could elevate her cherished Julian's standing in London society with a word.

The frustrated woman's hesitation was just long enough to make retreat impossible, for Lord and Lady Blakely themselves came out of the house wreathed in smiles to welcome their guests.

Lady St. James's fate was further sealed by the arrival of a new coach that contained a dazzling redhead who alighted daintily from the step with the assistance of a besotted gentleman and four half-grown, noisy children. The young people gave shrieks of joy and ran to surround Amy and Aggie.

Lionel examined the radiant, extravagantly dressed noblewoman with interest. He had recognized her at once, of course. The former Lady Madelyn Rathbone's face was almost as well known in London as the Prince Regent's. Her wedding to Mr. Langtry, a mere country gentleman of respectable but by no means lavish fortune saddled with four wards, had caused a sensation the previous spring, and their names rarely had been out of the social pages since. The wealthy couple and the gentleman's eldest ward had six estates between them that they visited by turns throughout the year like monarchs on royal progress.

No one had more influence in *ton* circles than Lady Madelyn. Only in her wildest imaginings could Lady St. James even *dream* of being accepted into the lady's social orbit. His stepmother's eyes glittered, reminding Lionel of a bird of prey that had sighted a particularly succulent morsel running tame on the ground.

"So good of you to come," Lady Blakely said, kissing the air above Lady St. James's cheek. Lionel's stepmother blinked, as if she had forgotten the viscountess's existence, which she probably had. "Will you not step into the parlor for some refreshments?"

It's a wonder, Lionel thought, that Lady Blakely didn't come away with frostbitten lips. Lady St. James's face was frozen in an expression probably meant to convey amiability, but Lionel thought the frightful grimace was quite enough to send small children shrieking to hide under their beds.

Lord Blakely shook hands with Lionel's father and gave Julian a friendly pat on the shoulder.

"You will no doubt have much to discuss with your son," he said genially. The look in his eyes made it more of a command than a passing comment. His message was clear; he would have no discord in his house.

Mary Ann gave her brother-in-law a look brimful of gratitude as he moved on to greet the new arrivals and positioned herself so she would be escorted inside with Julian on one arm and Melissa on the other.

That left Sir Andrew and Lionel facing each other so neatly that even Lionel doubted for a moment that it had been planned.

Lionel cautiously held out his hand, and after a short hesitation, his father grasped it with less than his old vigor.

"I hope I find you in good health, sir," Lionel said. To his dismay, his voice quavered slightly. His father was an irascible, unreasonable old tartar, but it smote Lionel to the soul to find him looking so old and brittle.

"Tolerable," Sir Andrew muttered gruffly. "You're looking . . . well."

Mary Ann leaned close to Melissa confidingly.

"Well, it's a start," Lionel distinctly heard her say.

Not if his stepmother had her way, Lionel thought, catching the venomous look Lady St. James cast in his direction before she composed her face for her introduction to Lady Madelyn.

It was a very good thing, Lionel thought, that looks truly could not kill.

As it was, Lionel thought it unfortunate that the employment of food tasters in great houses had fallen out of fashion.

Eleven

To Lionel's despair, the arrival of the formidable Earl of Stoneham and his sister, Lady Letitia, an influential hostess in her own right, put an end to his forlorn hope that Lady St. James would shake the dust of Leicestershire from her shoes and thus put an end to his discomfort.

With them, this influential couple had brought along Lord Lucas Renfield, a young lion in the House of Lords just rising to prominence who was, Lionel gathered from his hosts' warm welcome, a protégé of both Lord Stoneham's and Lord Blakely's. The gentleman's eyes had turned to frost when he saw Lionel, and even though they were slightly acquainted from evenings spent over the tables, he did not deign to acknowledge him, even after Mary Ann, noticing this, assumed he was unknown to Renfield and made a point of calling the young lion's attention to him for an introduction.

The fellow apparently had his standards, Lionel thought sourly as Renfield gave him a look of distaste and drew Mary Ann back, as if she were in danger of being soiled by him.

Mary Ann instantly extricated her arm from his hold and went to stand loyally by Lionel. She sent Lord Renfield a look that could have curdled milk.

"What can Blakely be thinking of to invite that fellow here?" Renfield said a moment later to the Earl of Stoneham in an undervoice Lionel knew he had been meant to overhear.

No, Lionel's stepmother would not budge a foot until she had exhausted every possibility for ingratiating herself with such luminaries, and Lionel was forced to witness the painful spectacle of Lady Letitia and Lady Madelyn enduring Lady St. James's unsubtle toad eating with well-bred tolerance but no enthusiasm. Lady St. James appeared oblivious to their polite attempts to extricate themselves; unless she received an outright snub, she would adhere to the unfortunate ladies like a sticking plaster.

Lionel should have enjoyed watching his stepmother make a fool of herself, but he only felt sad. Late that evening, when his father gently but firmly led her away from the sofa in the drawing room where Lady Letitia and Lady Madelyn had been subtly inching away from their would-be bosom bow, Lionel almost felt sorry for her.

This thought was so alarming that he immediately took himself off in search of a drink. He had entered Lord Blakely's library, where the ever-present decanter of brandy stood at the ready, and had actually pulled the cut-glass stopper when the image of Mary Ann's disappointed face that morning after finding him suffering from the effects of such self-indulgence popped into his head.

He took a deep breath and lowered the stopper back into the decanter, even though he could imagine the taste of the brandy on his tongue.

He wished he hadn't come.

His London lodgings might be cold and shabby. His way of life might be precarious at best. His lungs might be turning black with the constant influx of stale cigar smoke from gambling hells and toxic coal fumes from the filthy London air, but he could rub along night after night at the tables and not even notice that he was a lonely, pathetic husk of a man.

Mary Ann made him hope.

Mary Ann made him *want*.

He was better off without wanting.

He sat down at Blakely's desk and enjoyed the long shadows cast by the light from the fireplace. The servants must have built up the fire in anticipation of Lord Blakely's arrival now that the activities in the parlor were winding to a close for the evening, but the other lights in the room remained extinguished. Perhaps Blakely liked to sit here, too, in the semidarkness on winter nights.

Lionel took a deep breath and froze when a pair of fragrant feminine hands covered his eyes and a throaty giggle sounded in his ear. Apparently she had been hiding behind the chair, waiting to spring out at her victim.

He captured the lady's wrist and pulled her around to the side of his chair so he could see her.

He was not gentle.

"What the devil do you think you are doing, Barbara?" he demanded.

In the light of the fireplace he could see her voluptuous pink . . . charms were lovingly displayed in a low-cut white evening gown. It was not the one she had worn at dinner, although that one had been revealing enough. This one might as well have been a negligée for all the flesh it covered. Her hair, which had been arranged decorously on her head earlier in the evening, was now partially tumbling down her back, and she was surrounded, as usual, in a cloud of cloying French scent.

He took grim satisfaction in the way her pale blue eyes widened in startlement when she recognized him, but she recovered quickly.

"Lionel! How perfectly de trop you are! Go away! I have an assignation. I've sent him a note, and he should be here any minute."

"No doubt," he said dryly. "I suppose this charming little . . . surprise was intended for Lord Blakely. May I take leave to tell you, my dear girl, that—"

"Oh, Lionel, *darling,* don't be such an old poop! And I didn't *say* it was Lord Blakely. No one can accuse *me* of being indiscreet."

She reached out to touch his cheek but overbalanced, so he had to catch her in his arms to keep her from falling.

"Oooooh," she cooed, throwing her arms around him.

"None of that, my girl," he said, clenching his jaw as he tried to extricate himself and hold her upright at the same time. With a playful smirk, she pulled the knot of his carefully tied cravat and started to open his shirt.

"Stop it now," he hissed as he tried to avoid her juicily questing lips. From her sweet, plummy breath he could tell that his suspicions had been correct—the marchioness was quite thoroughly disguised. He should have known what she had in mind when she excused herself from the drawing room on the pretext of having a headache.

"Certainly, Lionel darling," she said agreeably. "After you kiss me for old time's sake."

"Deuce take it," he said, appalled by the prospect, and abruptly let go of her. She shrieked, fell on her voluptuous bottom with a resounding thump and began to cry.

"Shhhhh," Lionel said, regarding the closed door apprehensively. He was tempted to make good his escape, but he really couldn't leave her like this. What if one of the servants found her? Or Lord Blakely. Or his *wife!*

Then the fat would be in the fire. He couldn't leave even the faithless Barbara vulnerable to such humiliation.

"Up you go, there's a good girl," he said as he attempted to heave her to her feet.

"Now I'm all bruised," she said, looking back toward her injured posterior. A fatuous smile spread over her face. "Kiss it first and make it better," she said craftily.

"Barbara, you are very, very drunk," he said, enunciating clearly in the hope it would get through to her alcohol-fogged brain. "Let's get you to bed so you can sleep it off."

"I don't want to go to bed," she pouted. She let her knees buckle so he had to deal with her dead weight. "It's *lonely* there." She licked her lips. "Unless you would like to join me—"

"My dear," he said with a glimmer of humor in spite of himself. The whole situation was so ridiculous. He finally succeeded in pulling her upright. "Don't be absurd."

"I'm cold," she complained, trying to snuggle into his arms. "The least you can do is keep me warm."

Lionel snorted and removed his coat to put it around her shoulders. She angrily cast it off and let it drop onto the floor.

"You are so cruel to me, Lionel," she said. Her lower lip was quavering. "All I want is a little affection."

"You already have a dog," he said dryly. "Come along. I'll sneak you up to your room by the back stairs before someone sees you."

"Why shouldn't someone see me?" she shouted belligerently. "I'm perfectly respectable, which is more than I can say for you!"

"Shhhhh," he said warningly. "Do you want to rouse the whole house? Come along, now."

Before he could get her moving, Lord Blakely walked briskly into the room and stopped dead in his tracks.

"What in blazes is going on here, St. James?" he barked.

"Oh, come off your high ropes, man," Lionel said in exasperation. "And keep your voice down unless you want an audience."

"Alexander," Barbara cooed, reaching for him. The viscount flinched backward with comical haste.

"Lady Cavenish planned a nice little surprise for you,"

Lionel said with mock cheerfulness, "but I'm afraid I came in before you and spoiled it."

"The devil you say!" Blakely exclaimed, looking properly horrified. "Get her out of here, St. James! Vanessa could come in any moment. She often joins me here in the evenings."

Barbara bounded forward and threw her arms around the viscount in girlish enthusiasm.

"Lady Cavenish, I believe I made it abundantly clear a year ago in London that your attentions, while flattering, are entirely unwelcome," he said, leaning back as she draped herself over his chest. He caught her shoulders and attempted to hold her at bay. She had a silly smile on her face, and her head lolled on her shoulder. "You are laboring under a grave misapprehension if you think that I—"

"You're losing her, Blakely," Lionel said dryly as Barbara's eyes glazed over and she started to sag.

"Bloody hell," Blakely said, most improperly, as he shook Barbara by the shoulders. "Lady Cavenish, *please!* Don't pass out now, I beg of you!"

The marchioness raised her head and smiled blearily at him.

"Lady Cavenish, Alexander?" she said in gentle reproach. "We are closer friends than that, I hope."

"Barbara, then," he said hastily, looking relieved. Lionel shared this sentiment. There was no discreet way to convey an unconscious woman up two flights of stairs at nine o'clock in the evening. "Come along, now, Barbara, let us get you to your room—"

His words died at the sound of a knock on the door.

"Alexander?" a cheerful, feminine voice called out.

"It's Vanessa," he hissed helplessly at Lionel. He looked at the woman in his arms in consternation. "How will I ever explain—"

The knock came again.

Lionel rolled his eyes and prepared to make the ultimate sacrifice. He had been trying to disabuse Mary Ann and her sisters of their misguided notion that he was some sort of knight errant. *This* should do the trick nicely.

"Get behind the chair," Lionel whispered. Blakely gave him a grateful look and dove for cover as Lionel put his arm around Barbara to keep her from following him. Fortunately, Barbara accepted the exchange of supporting male bodies without complaint.

Blakely just managed to crouch down out of sight before the door opened.

"Alexander, darling," Lady Blakely said airily as she and a smiling Mary Ann sailed into the room. "Mary Ann and I have had the most delightful idea! How would it be if tomorrow—"

The smiles died on both the ladies' faces as they stopped dead and stared.

Lionel shuddered to imagine what they were thinking. Here he was, in his shirtsleeves, with half of his chest exposed by his opened shirt, clinging to a weaving, scantily clad woman to keep her from sliding into a drunken heap on the floor.

The ladies looked so distressed that he completely forgot his intention of letting them think he was sunk in a veritable pit of depravity.

"Lady Blakely, Miss Whittaker. This isn't what it seems," Lionel blurted out.

Mary Ann's eyes looked straight into his.

"Is it not, Mr. St. James?" she asked with a little catch in her voice that broke his heart. "What precisely *is* it, then?"

Lionel looked from Mary Ann's eyes to Lady Blakely's embarrassed face. Lady Blakely put a consoling arm around her younger sister's shoulders and gave Lionel a reproachful look.

Barbara gave a long, throaty laugh.

"Yes, Lionel, darling," she said drunkenly. "What precisely *is* it?"

Well, she had him there.

What could he say? That this abundant, perfumed package was not intended for him, but for Lady Blakely's devoted husband? He could almost feel poor Blakely shaking in his boots from his hiding place behind the chair.

Blakely had more to lose from being implicated in this sordid little scene than Lionel did.

Much more.

"Lady Cavenish," he said carefully, "has had a bit too much to drink."

"Very *good,* darling," Barbara tittered, as if he had made a brilliant deduction. Looking straight into Mary Ann's eyes, she snuggled against Lionel with a smug look on her face. "If you'll excuse us," she said, licking her lips, "Lionel is about to take me to bed."

"No," he said, suddenly visited by inspiration. "I am about to call your *maid* to take you to bed." He appealed to Lady Blakely. "We can't let anyone see her like this."

"I should rather think not," she said faintly. "Mary Ann, will you please fetch Lady Cavenish's maid? Tell her that Lady Cavenish has taken ill and requires her assistance at once."

Mary Ann bit her lip and left the room. Lionel took an involuntary step after her, but Lady Blakely laid a hand on his arm to stop him.

"Mr. St. James," she said deliberately, "your private amusements are, of course, none of my business, but my children and young sisters reside in this house, and I would protect them from . . . sights such as these."

"I assure you, Lady Blakely—" he began.

"Mr. St. James," she said, raising a slightly shaking hand to cut him off. He could hardly bear the disappointment in her eyes. "I do not think there is anything more to be said."

Lionel felt a wave of compassion sweep over him.

Better that Lady Blakely should think the worst of *him* than have doubts about her husband's fidelity.

As for Mary Ann . . . Mary Ann had always been lost to him.

"No, my lady," he said gently. "There is not."

Twelve

"How *could* you?" demanded Mary Ann, hands on hips, the next morning when she confronted Lionel on his way to breakfast. It was obvious she had been laying in wait for him.

"I never claimed to be a saint," he said, attempting to forestall what promised from her stormy eyes to be a painful scene by edging around her.

She grabbed his arm.

"Well, you certainly are determined to act like one."

This stopped him in his tracks.

"I beg your pardon?" he asked, certain he could not have heard her correctly.

"Do you think I believed for one moment that you would lower yourself to . . ." she gulped, and her voice trailed off as if what she meant to say was so distasteful to her that she couldn't say the words. "With that dreadful woman?" she finished lamely.

"You believed. I saw your face."

"Maybe right at first, when she was in your arms and it was such a shock. But later, when I was calmer, I thought it through. You are covering for Alexander, of course."

Lionel drew himself to his full height and regarded her with the mocking smile that never failed to intimidate his opponents when he played cards.

"And what, may I ask, has brought you to this extraordinary conclusion?"

"Do not attempt to bamboozle *me,* Lionel St. James," she said, poking his chest with a sharp finger. "I, who have seen your kindness."

"Kindness, is it?" He shook his head. "My dear girl, do come out of the clouds."

"If you were going to have an assignation with a lady, you certainly wouldn't choose Alexander's library, where anyone might come upon you."

"Perhaps the prospect of being discovered adds to the excitement," he said provocatively.

To his surprise, she did not pursue this red herring. Instead, she gave his chest another hard poke.

"She was there to meet Alexander, as you suggested earlier. I had the whole from Alexander last night, so do not bother to deny it."

Now she *had* surprised him. Had Alexander *admitted* to her that he was having an affair with Lady Cavenish?

"Listen to me, Miss Whittaker," he said sternly. "This is none of your affair."

"You are protecting him and *her* at the risk of your own reputation. It isn't the first time, is it?"

He gave a snort of humorless laughter.

"I suppose you think you know what you are talking about."

"After knowing you and meeting her, do you think I believe you abducted her against her will? Not that I ever *did,* mind!"

She was getting far too close to the truth.

"Do *not* pursue this!" he said, grasping her shoulders and giving her a little shake. "Think of your family and leave well enough alone."

Mary Ann's eyes narrowed.

"Do you think Alexander is guilty, then? Do you honestly think that he and that woman—You *do,* don't you?"

"Well, you said he had admitted the truth to you—"

"He said she tried to force herself upon him a year ago in London, but he refused her advances and he thought she had lost interest until she pursued him here."

"Then he is completely innocent of any wrongdoing," he asserted.

"Innocent of any wrongdoing, is he?" Mary Ann exclaimed. "Hardly! How *could* he let everyone think *you* are consorting with that wretched hussy?"

"Better for them to think it of me and not of *him*. I have much less to lose than he does."

"Why will Alexander simply not tell Vanessa the truth, then, that Lady Barbara is after him, with no encouragement whatsoever on his part?"

Lionel rolled his eyes. This girl was *too* innocent.

"Because she would never believe him," he said in exasperation. "No wife would."

"Vanessa would," Mary Ann said confidently. "She loves him."

"That has nothing to do with it. Trust me. If your sister catches wind of the fact that Lady Cavenish is pursuing her husband, she will assume he is guilty."

"Nonsense! Why *should* she?"

Lionel threw up his hands in exasperation.

"Because she is a *wife!* Most wives expect their husbands to have affairs, and they simply look the other way. But the marriage is never the same again because the trust that lay at its foundation is gone forever. After a period of time, it occurs to the wife that if her husband can betray his vows, so can she. Before long they are both taking lovers and merely enduring one another's company on social occasions. I have seen it happen time and time again."

"He made me promise not to tell her the truth," Mary Ann said with a dejected sigh. "I thought he was going to cry. It was . . . unnerving."

"I am not surprised," Lionel said dryly. He was still

not completely convinced of Blakely's innocence. Would Lady Cavenish have pursued him into Leicestershire without *some* encouragement? "I have never seen a man so firmly under the cat's paw as your precious brother-in-law."

"He is *not* under the cat's paw," she objected. "He loves her."

Lionel caressed her soft cheek with the palm of his hand. He couldn't help himself.

"It is the same thing. Do not worry about me, sweetheart," he said wryly. "I haven't a good name to lose, after all."

"Lady St. James has already been at Alexander to cast you from the house."

"My stepmother?" Lionel exclaimed in dismay. "How did *she* become acquainted with this shameful business?"

"Apparently Lady Cavenish's maid was gossiping about the affair below stairs, and the whole house is humming with speculation. It is most unfortunate."

Lionel sighed. He might have known Barbara would employ an indiscreet maid.

And Barbara, unless he missed his guess, had already come up with a highly colored version of the incident that portrayed her, once again, as the innocent victim of rampant male lust in order to excuse her own reckless behavior. He supposed he was to have plied her with liquor so he could have his wicked way with her.

"I have been waiting here to go in with you to breakfast," Mary Ann said hesitantly. "I thought you would welcome the support."

Lionel looked down into her earnest face. She was such a darling. She really did believe she could defend him from the acrimony of both their families.

He could not spurn her, even though he hesitated to expose her to censure by allowing her to champion him.

It might be his last opportunity to have the lovely Mary Ann on his arm, after all, he thought ruefully.

"Let us face the lions, then," he said with a wry smile as he crooked his elbow in invitation.

All conversation stopped when *that rake* and Mary Ann entered the room.

Vanessa's heart was filled with indignation. How *could* he disport himself in her home as if he were in some dockyard pleasure house after all the kindness she and her family had shown him?

And how could Mary Ann side with him when she had witnessed his shocking behavior with that woman last night?

Vanessa was not the sort of person to judge people, but even *she* had to believe the evidence of her own eyes! Naturally Mary Ann was attracted to the handsome rogue, but surely she knew it would do her reputation no good to associate with him.

She could have wept with frustration. He was *ruining* her house party!

Lady St. James looked as if she smelled something sour and Lady Cavenish, looking conscious, put a hand to her heaving bosom and fixed him with apprehensive eyes, as if she feared he might renew his amorous attack on her person.

Alexander had warned her in the beginning that the gamester was not a man who should be brought into the bosom of their family, and she should have listened to him.

Melissa St. James's cheeks were spotted with high color; her brother, Julian, stared at his half brother as if he would dearly love to hit him. Everyone else determinedly resumed their conversations in an apparent attempt to cover the awkwardness.

Where *was* Alexander when Vanessa needed his support?

Even though Lionel St. James was in her black books at the moment, Vanessa could *not* let a guest stand on the threshold like that. She greeted him politely but coolly. She fixed her eyes on Mary Ann and gestured for her to join their sisters. It was Vanessa's duty, as hostess, to take charge of Mr. St. James. Not her unmarried sister's.

After all, Lord Stoneham and Lady Letitia would be down any minute, and Vanessa couldn't bear for their disapproval to fall on Mary Ann. Lady Letitia, especially, was inclined to think Vanessa and her sisters inferior in breeding, and it was only with great difficulty that the great lady resigned herself to having her nephew's blood mingle with that of the lowly Whittakers.

But worse, her mother would soon be down, and she would have a fit of the vapors if Mary Ann alienated Julian St. James's parents. Her latest scheme to marry off her middle daughter creditably depended upon their approval of the girl.

She might have known that instead of taking the hint to disassociate herself with the disgraced man, Mary Ann would set her jaw and escort him to the chafing dishes, fill a plate for him and pour him a cup of coffee. Then she sat beside him at the far end of the table, away from the others, and returned their looks, glare for glare, like a mother bear defending her cub.

Her stare into Lady Cavenish's eyes might just as well have been a declaration of war.

"Melissa," hissed Lady St. James when her daughter stood up.

Head held high but with her face flaming, Melissa came to sit on the other side of her half brother.

Lionel was unbelievably touched.

His little sister could not possibly know the truth, yet

she, like Mary Ann, was willing to risk the edge of her mother's sharp tongue to side with him.

He had no doubt that censure would be most unpleasant for her. Lady St. James gave her daughter a poisonous stare, and Lionel's father placed a reassuring hand over Lady Cavenish's, as if to give her courage.

To Lionel, this was the unkindest cut of all.

It was clear that his father had swallowed whatever outrageous tale of his culpability Barbara had fed him.

What else had he expected? Lionel thought bleakly. His heart turned over when Mary Ann's younger sisters picked up their plates and joined him and Mary Ann at the end of the table, even though they could not possibly have the least idea why he was being shunned by the rest of the company.

Lionel might have disgraced himself yet again, giving credence to his stepmother's oft-repeated declaration that he did not know how to behave around decent people, but this time he wasn't alone and friendless.

"It was dreadful. Simply dreadful," Vanessa told Alexander in the privacy of her boudoir when she went up to change her clothes. He had appeared in her doorway after a bruising morning ride that had done little to exorcise the demons from his guilty conscience.

Ordinarily Alexander considered it his duty to provide a hospitable presence over the breakfast cups when they had guests, but, like a coward, he had avoided the inevitable spectacle of Lionel being ostracized in his place.

His hair was disheveled, his boots were muddy and he probably smelled strongly of horse and sweat, but he could not resist the compulsion to take Vanessa into his arms and blurt out the truth. He had never lied to her. How could he have thought he could do so now?

When he reached for her, though, she put a hand to his chest.

"Alexander, we must talk," she said, evading his lips when he would have kissed her.

His heart sank like a stone. She had *never* refused to kiss him. Not since the day she married him.

Did she suspect?

Could she *know?*

Lionel would keep his secret. But Mary Ann might tell her sister the truth, that it was Alexander that Lady Cavenish had intended to seduce last night. It would be so much better coming from him.

Even now, Vanessa might assume he was guilty of having an affair with Lady Cavenish because he didn't own up right away. He should have stood his ground instead of seizing the convenient escape Lionel gave him. Hiding behind the desk was the act of a coward—and a guilty man.

"Perhaps you *should* have a word with Mr. St. James," she said carefully. "His stepmother may be right after all."

Alexander stifled an exhalation of relief. This was about Lady St. James's request that he expel Lionel from the house.

But he couldn't. He just *couldn't.* Not even to save his own skin.

"Vanessa, I told you last night that I don't believe what happened is his fault," he said carefully.

"You know how I feel about *that,*" she scoffed.

He did, indeed.

She had made it clear on more than one occasion, when an erring husband tried to place the blame for his indiscretion on the female who tempted him, that in her opinion even the boldest woman would not attempt to seduce a man unless he had indicated his willingness to dally with her.

The thing Alexander treasured most about their marriage was the perfect trust that existed between them. Vanessa would not be one of those complacent wives willing to turn a blind eye to her husband's peccadilloes as long as he acted the role of a devoted consort in public and supported her in the style to which she had become accustomed.

If Vanessa thought he was having an affair with another woman, she would leave him.

He was sure of it.

Regardless of the scandal—regardless of the fact that she didn't have a penny of her own to her name—she would leave him and starve in a ditch rather than sleep another night under his roof.

And even if he managed to persuade her to stay for the sake of their sons, she wouldn't love him anymore.

"I wish we could rid the house of Lady Cavenish as well," she was saying, "but we can hardly do so without offending Sir Andrew and Lady St. James. Perhaps if you talked to him man-to-man and convinced him it would be better for all concerned if he left—"

"Invite the man to spend the holidays with us and then show him the door?" he asked incredulously. "This is not like you, Vanessa."

She took an agitated turn about the room.

"I don't know what to do," she said, looking tearful. "The whole situation is just so *hideous*. Our Christmas will be quite spoilt."

"No, it won't, my love," he said, filled with self-loathing. "We will still have each other."

"You are right," she said, looking up at him with a sweet, brave smile.

Alexander's arms closed around her as she laid her head against his chest and hugged his waist. He savored the fragrance of orange blossom, the scent she had worn since before their courtship.

He couldn't live without her. He had to make her understand.

Tell her!

"You are my rock," she said. Her words were muffled against his chest.

For God's sake, tell her!

"Vanessa—" he began, determined to make a clean breast of it.

She looked up at him with those lovely blue eyes of hers.

"I thank heaven every day that you have never given me the kind of anxiety other women have to tolerate from their husbands," she said earnestly. "I don't know what I would do if I couldn't depend upon your absolute loyalty and strength."

Alexander closed his eyes as she raised her face for his kiss and was weak.

Thirteen

"I'm leaving Giles," the spoiled, ungrateful creature said.

It was only by clenching her hands into fists so hard that her nails scored her palms that Lady St. James was able to stop herself from slapping her younger sister silly.

Barbara was in her boudoir, wrapped in a costly cashmere bedjacket and reclining voluptuously on a satin counterpane. Naturally the marchioness was given Lady Blakely's most luxurious guest suite, for hostesses always deferred to rank in such matters.

This was only one of the countless privileges Barbara would forfeit if she lost her head and threw away the marriage that Beatrice had worked so untiringly to procure for her.

Tears scored the marchioness's pale cheeks as they slipped from her reddened eyes, and her hair was tangled about her face like a witch's, yet still Barbara was beautiful. Some women—Beatrice, for example—looked so hideous when they wept that they gave gentlemen a positive disgust for them, but not her wretched younger sister! At such moments, susceptible men would give Barbara the earth, sun and stars if such trifling baubles would make her smile again.

Beatrice, however, felt only resentment.

"Are you *mad?*" Beatrice shouted. "I wouldn't be able

to hold my head up in society again if you did anything so stupid."

Anger made Barbara a fraction less lovely as she sat up to face her sister.

"That's all you care about, isn't it? *Your* standing in the world," she said accusingly. "To elevate our family—to elevate *you*—*my* happiness must be sacrificed—"

"How *dare* you say that to me? I, who have made you a marchioness! I suppose you would rather be living in squalor with my loathsome rogue of a stepson!"

"Lionel *loved* me!" she cried. *"He* would not have humiliated me by consorting with trollops!"

"What is *that* to the point?" Beatrice said in exasperation. "It's not as if *you* have been as pure as the driven snow when it comes to taking lovers outside marriage."

"If Giles were not such a rotter, I would not desire lovers!"

"Nonsense!" Beatrice had nothing but contempt for this specious reasoning. *"All* marriages pall after awhile."

"Not Lord Blakely's marriage, it seems," Barbara said bitterly. "I was practically buttered and served to him on a gilded platter last night, but he refused me. *Me!* What does the man *want?"*

"Not you, obviously." Beatrice did not even try to suppress a glimmer of smug satisfaction. "I hope your head pains you *very* much for the mischief you might have caused! You were supposed to charm and flatter Lord Blakely so he would look kindly on Julian, not assault the man half naked in his library! Are you trying to ruin all of us?"

"There's a picture," Barbara said wistfully. "The divine Alexander half naked. It was no such thing, more's the pity."

"You know what I mean! And I'll thank you to avoid playing such tricks in the future! It's bad enough the whole household suspects you of having an affair with that disgusting stepson of mine. *Will* the creature never leave me in peace? Seeing him has Andrew thinking about the past and looking melancholy again."

Barbara gave a sigh of what might have been regret.

"I have only a dim memory of last night," she said, "but one fact came through with painful clarity. Lionel was disgusted by my behavior. He *pitied* me. He was no more tempted than Lord Blakely to take advantage of . . . the situation."

She rose and went over to a small mirror flanked by gilded cupids and examined her face carefully.

"Perhaps some Milk of Roses—" she said, sounding anxious.

Beatrice gave an unladylike shriek of exasperation.

"To Perdition with your outrageous vanity, Barbara! You have seriously jeopardized our welcome in this house, just when Julian's future most depends upon our family giving a good impression. Do you think Lady Blakely will have Julian anywhere *near* her husband—or any of us, for that matter—if she thinks that you are playing your games with Lord Blakely?"

Barbara gave a sniff of contempt.

"Lady Blakely is so busy with her house and her guests and her brats that she has little time to spend on her husband."

"There you're wrong, my girl," Beatrice said. "Lady Blakely is no fool, for all that she came from nothing. If you know what's good for you, you'll continue to let Lionel be the villain in this affair *and* forget this foolishness of leaving your husband. If you think you will continue to enjoy invitations to the most select parties once you no longer have the prestige of your husband's name and title to lend you consequence, you are much mistaken."

"Not even my own sister loves me for myself," Barbara said in a small, hurt voice.

Beatrice gave a snort of disgust at this blatant self-pity.

"And whose fault is *that,* pray?" Beatrice asked impatiently. If Beatrice were the wife of a marquess, *she* certainly wouldn't be lolling about like a pampered, lachrymose cow, whining about her misfortunes.

But, no. The best Beatrice could do was a mere baronet, who came burdened with a surly, abominably spoiled heir into the bargain. Ten years after Beatrice thought the wretched creature was out of her life, he was *still* plaguing her.

"So your husband has taken a mistress or two!" she told her sister. "Why should *you* be singularly blessed among women with a husband whose eyes never stray?"

Actually, to Beatrice's knowledge Andrew had never transgressed with other women, but the way he invariably had placed his son's wishes before those of his wife in the early days of their marriage was almost as bad. If she had gotten her way, the brat would have been sent to boarding school before their marriage lines were dry.

There were many kinds of betrayal, and Beatrice doubted that any husband was guiltless of them all. A lady of breeding simply clung to her dignity and waited for the man to come to his senses, as Andrew, albeit reluctantly when faced with his son's treachery, eventually did.

"I cannot discern what it is about Lady Blakely that exerts such power over a man like that," Barbara was saying as she licked her lips and pursed them coquettishly to study the effect in the mirror. "I'm of a mind to wipe that smug, complacent look off her face by demonstrating that *no* husband remains faithful forever."

Jarred back to the present, Beatrice fixed her beautiful sister with a determined stare.

"You will do nothing of the kind, you little wretch! The entire household is inclined to blame my scapegrace of a stepson for last night's scandalous episode. Let them, for pity's sake! It ties the whole thing up rather neatly. Your reputation, such as it is, is somewhat salvaged. And Andrew, who has been entertaining regrets for banishing Lionel, has had his past action justified by this new evidence of the boy's perfidy. Julian, by contrast, is bound to look like a veritable Galahad."

She gave a harsh shrill of laughter.

"Perhaps I should thank you for losing your head last night. I can think of nothing more likely to convince my cherished spouse that *my* son, rather than his firstborn, is the more worthy to be his heir."

Barbara's eyes narrowed.

"And people think *I* am the wicked sister," she said accusingly.

Beatrice gave her a hard look.

"I am a good mother seeing to the welfare of her children, which is more than I can say for you!"

Barbara's face turned a dull red and she looked down in what might have been shame. At least the little wretch felt *some* remorse at leaving her children behind while she pursued her life of pleasure.

Seeing her sister cowed at last, Beatrice favored her with a tight smile.

Barbara was as unprincipled as she was beautiful. And as self-serving.

Angry as she was with Beatrice, Barbara would not disclose her own reprehensible betrayal of Lady Blakely's hospitality in striving to seduce her husband—not while there was still a chance of attracting that gentleman's ardor and attention.

Barbara had always been possessed of a dangerous fondness for Lionel, but she would not let *that* stand in the way of her own interests. Beatrice wouldn't be surprised if Barbara meant to take Lionel as her lover as well.

If so, Beatrice had no objection as long as Barbara didn't jeopardize her ambition for Julian or compromise the standing of her family in society. Beatrice could not approve of her sister's seemingly boundless appetite for romantic intrigue, but she had no hesitation in exploiting it if it served her purpose.

For a moment, Lionel thought he had walked into a brick wall.

From his prone position on the stable floor, he looked up and squinted to bring the blurry image into focus.

What he found almost made him close his eyes again.

"Hallo, Julian," he said dryly as he gingerly touched his stinging jaw. "Not a bad right cross, old boy. My felicitations."

"Get up, you scoundrel," his half brother said through clenched teeth.

"Not if you are going to hit me again." Lionel relaxed his fists and reminded himself that it is vastly unsporting to pound a fatter and slower man into submission.

"It's no more than you deserve," Julian snarled. "How *could* you force yourself on my Aunt Barbara? Have you no shame?"

Lionel picked up his hat, brushed the straw off and rose to his feet so he could tower over his brother.

"Don't be a slowtop, Julian. You must know the fair Barbara hardly needs any forcing at all if a gentleman is so inclined."

For a moment Lionel thought Julian was going to hit him again, but the boy's natural sense of justice apparently prevailed.

"You are absolutely right, Lionel," Julian said, exhaling a long, tension-filled breath. "I have been wanting to hit you for a long time, and Aunt Barbara's virtue was just a convenient excuse." He gave Lionel a rueful half smile. "It felt good, I must admit. Even if I may have broken my knuckles on your stubborn jaw."

"Why?" Lionel asked, rubbing his chin. "You haven't seen me for ten years."

"Exactly!" Julian said. "Why did you have to come back into my life *now?* I might have made a decent impression on Lord Blakely and been offered the vacant post as his secretary. I'm a scholarly, clerkly sort of person, for all that my parents sneer at such bourgeois qualities. The post is beneath me, my mother insists, but it would give me a little independence. At last I would be free of my mother's hectoring and my father's disappointed looks because I'm not a bloody paragon like you."

"Like *me!* I can't imagine anything he would want less."

"But *no,*" Julian continued, giving Lionel a hard look at the interruption. *"You* had to be here, looking dashing and debonair, and charming all the ladies. My chances with Miss Whittaker were slim before, but with *you* on the scene, she's forgotten that I exist."

"Are you in love with her?" Lionel asked, forcing down the feelings of jealousy that made him want to grab his brother by the throat.

Julian gave him an incredulous look.

"I hardly know her. But she's a very good sort of girl, and she makes me laugh. Melissa likes her, too, and could come to live with us after we're married. I have to marry *someone,* now that I'm the heir." He gave Lionel an accusing look. "There aren't too many girls that Mother approves of who would look twice at a slug like me."

"You are *not* a slug," Lionel said, because he could not bear the sadness in his brother's eyes.

Julian gave an unhappy sigh.

"You're wrong there. I am not a bruising rider or a deadly marksman, and I don't possess a sense of style. My father almost bought me a pair of colors before peace was declared in order to make a man of me, did you know that?"

He shuddered eloquently.

"I assume your affectionate mother put an end to *that* notion!" Lionel said with a dry bark of laughter.

Julian's cheeks turned a dull red, which confirmed that Lionel was correct in his assumption.

"It takes more to be a man than good bottom on horseback and a lot of swaggering," Lionel said, feeling sorry for his younger brother despite the fact that his jaw might be broken. It hurt like the very devil.

Julian turned away and hunched one shoulder.

"I should think *so,* not that Father would entertain such an enlightened opinion," he said angrily. "How *could* you leave us to their tender mercies! It has been just as bad for Melissa, for she missed you terribly. You know what they are! Without you to draw their fire, they were both at me day and night. Everyone seems to think it's a great thing to be the heir, but I can tell you it has fairly well ruined my life! I wanted to go into the church or law. But, no! I have to beat my head against the wall trying to distinguish the family name, and it's all *your* fault! My mother has political ambitions for me, if you please. Can you see *me* addressing Parliament?"

Julian took another deep breath and, incredibly, gave his brother a rueful smile. For an instant, Lionel saw the sweet, good-natured brother he remembered in that smile.

"That's why I hit you," Julian said in a small voice.

"I'm sorry," Lionel said, at a loss. He had just assumed Julian would *like* being the heir to their father's fortune. *He* had certainly reveled in the role while it lasted. Lionel had been so caught up in his own feelings of betrayal, he hadn't even thought of how turning his back on his family would affect Julian and Melissa. *They* would always be taken care of, he had assumed, because they shared *her* blood. And Lionel honestly thought his absence would bring peace to the contentious household, since he would no longer be going head-to-head with his manipulative stepmother.

Apparently he had been mistaken. Could Mary Ann be right about his family needing him?

"What really happened with Aunt Barbara?" Julian asked shrewdly.

"I'm sure you've heard the tale," Lionel said, looking down. "It was all over the house this morning."

"You're the kind of cad who would force himself on a lady who isn't . . . herself at the moment?"

"Certainly," Lionel said flippantly. "Can you doubt it? Now, if you will excuse me—"

"I've seen you with the ladies," Julian persisted. "And that doesn't wash. You are chivalrous to the point of imbecility. You always have been. All a woman has to do is shed a single tear and you're falling all over yourself to do her bidding."

"Perhaps I've changed," Lionel said, walking past Julian toward Thunder's stall. "You don't know me anymore."

"I never did believe you abducted Aunt Barbara," Julian said. "Neither did Melissa. We tried to tell Mother that, but she refused to listen. So did Father."

Before he could think better of it, Lionel turned and put an affectionate hand on his brother's shoulder. Julian shrugged it away and averted his face.

"Thank you for that, Julian," Lionel said quietly.

"She concocted that Cheltenham tragedy to save her reputation when she got caught in the act so she could still marry the marquess. And you, gallant bastard that you are, let her blacken your reputation instead."

"Julian, no good will come of raking up that old scandal. The lady is married now. And she is not a happy woman, for all the honors she possesses as the wife of a great man."

"I knew it! You *are* protecting her."

"What absolute drivel," Lionel said with a creditable sneer. "Why should I?"

"Yours is not the only life she has ruined. Did you know that? She makes quite a habit of setting her sights on some unfortunate fellow, teasing him until he is mad with love for her, and then abandoning him to his fate. You were merely her first victim."

"That's a very pretty story, Julian," Lionel said deliberately. "I think you have been listening to idle gossip. It is not an attractive trait in a gentleman, and your darling Mama would not approve."

"Confound it, Lionel!"

"This discussion is *over*, Brother," Lionel said firmly. "I am going for a ride on Thunder. You may accompany me or not, as you wish, as long as Lady Cavenish is *not* the subject of our conversation."

"I would like that very much," said Julian, looking up at Lionel with the almost worshipful pale blue eyes of the endearing little boy he once had been.

Lady St. James was ready to scream with frustration as she sat helplessly in Lady Blakely's parlor, sipping tea with the other ladies and watching her grown daughter disgrace herself.

For once, Melissa was impervious to her subtle winks and hints as she joined a handful of ill-behaved girls in their shrieking and jostling high spirits at one end of the large room.

Never would Beatrice have tolerated such behavior from her own children before guests when they were small. They never saw the inside of Beatrice's parlor except for short, correct appearances before guests, as was proper. Yet here were Lady Blakely and her mother smiling with what appeared to be fond approval as the girls giggled and laughed and generally conducted themselves like perfect little hoydens.

Worst of all, her boy, her precious boy, had once again placed himself under the influence of that *rogue*. Before long he would be smoking those dreadful cheroots and disporting himself with the loathsome creatures that inhabited the gutters of London.

The two young men had come in laughing from a ride together, and, in an excess of high spirits Beatrice could only deplore, regaled the assembled company with tales of their youthful exploits. The other ladies laughed with amusement at narratives that rendered Beatrice positively white-faced with horror.

Lady St. James hadn't the remotest idea that a much younger Julian and Melissa had leapt from the nursery window onto the roof of a lower floor to climb down to the ground via a convenient tree when she had confined them to their rooms for bad behavior.

She would have died a thousand deaths if she'd known how close her darlings had come to being broken on the ground beside her flower garden. She would never be able to look at her roses again without shuddering.

Beatrice knew very well whom to blame for these dangerous exploits—Lionel, their leader in all things wicked and disobedient. Of themselves, Julian and Melissa would never have dared such a thing.

Without Lionel to lead them astray, her children were easily guided, eager-to-please pattern cards of decorum. Most of the time.

Now, instead of doing his best to ingratiate himself with Lord Blakely and capture the heart of Miss Whittaker, who Beatrice was certain would make him a charming, suitably submissive wife, he was cutting up larks with his half brother, and the two of them were making Melissa whoop with unbecoming laughter.

This, after Lady St. James strictly forbade her daughter

to have anything more to do with her dreadful half brother. Beatrice had nearly died of mortification when Melissa defied her wishes to stand with the disgraced man at breakfast that morning. The tongue-lashing she had been compelled to administer to her errant daughter obviously had left no impression at all.

Julian even forgot himself so far as to form what appeared to be a fast friendship with Matthew, the youngest Langtry child, after he and Lord Blakely's twin sons were admitted—very improperly, in Lady St. James's opinion—to the parlor with their dog.

The sight of Julian lolling on the floor in a mad tangle of grubby little boys, teaching the dog how to perform tricks for the children's amusement, was hardly edifying!

What must their hosts *think* of them? And with Lady Letitia and Lady Madelyn, two of the most influential hostesses of the *ton,* present, too.

Fortunately for small blessings, at least Miss Whittaker was spared the spectacle of Julian wallowing about on the floor with the children like a beached whale.

But not for long.

Julian was still on the ground with the dog's paws captured in his hands when the girl came tripping into the room with Lord Blakely and Mr. Langtry at her heels.

"It is snowing," she cried out joyfully. "Hurry up! Get your warm clothes on and prepare for a snowball fight to end all snowball fights!"

Just as she feared, Melissa jumped up from the sofa and took Lionel's free arm as he unceremoniously hoisted his brother to his feet as if he weighed nothing.

The four of them left the room arm-in-arm, deaf to her protests, as they swept the children out of the house before them.

"Mary Ann," called Mrs. Whittaker plaintively to the empty air. "You have only four hours to get ready for the ball! And you might catch a chill!"

She and Beatrice exchanged a look of commiseration.

"I am persuaded you must think this very odd, Lady Madelyn," Beatrice said with an apologetic laugh as Lady Madelyn stood staring thoughtfully after them.

"Not at all," she said, favoring Beatrice with a brilliant smile. "A snowball fight! How delightful!"

She turned to her husband.

"Remember our first snowball fight, darling?" she asked that boyishly grinning gentleman as she held her hand out to him.

"Forever, my love," he whispered as he kissed her knuckles. "Come along now, or we shall miss all the fun."

With a sigh of resignation, Beatrice resumed her seat and picked up her tepid tea. What else could she do, after all, when everyone in the house seemed to be out of their minds?

The remaining ladies didn't even flinch when a juicy snowball hit the window.

"Look at the discord Lionel has caused in this household," Lady St. James complained to her husband in the privacy of their bedchamber as she paced the floor in agitation. "He has caused one scandal here by forcing himself on poor Barbara. And now he is leading Julian into boisterous behavior. Julian has only this one chance to make a good impression on Lord Blakely and the earl. Lionel is ruining *everything!*"

"I will speak to him," Sir Andrew said, looking determined. "He must not be allowed to blacken our name further."

"I do not think that would be wise," Beatrice said in alarm. The *last* thing she wanted was for her husband to have a heart-to-heart talk with his firstborn. Ten years of living on the outermost fringes of society had not dulled Lionel's charm; rather, his disreputable life had given him an air of mystery that both men and women found most attractive. He was strong, now, and handsome. It would not take much for the creature to revive the affection his father had never lost for him. Beatrice was uncomfortably aware that her own, infinitely more satisfactory son had never taken Lionel's place in his father's heart. "Rather, you should speak to Lord Blakely and ask him to—"

"I do not like to put our host in such a position," Andrew said, patting his wife's hand. "Do not be so concerned, my love."

"You must not believe a word he says," she blurted out.

Andrew smiled sadly at her.

"My dear, I have no delusions about my son's character, I assure you," he said as he left the room.

But you have hope, Beatrice thought apprehensively. *I can see it in your eyes.*

Fourteen

Lionel scooped up another handful of the soft, wet snow and looked about for a likely target. With the deadly aim for which he once was famous at Manton's, he set his sights on his brother's tall hat of curly beaver and watched with satisfaction as it toppled from his head.

Then he grinned and taunted Julian until his half brother was forced to retaliate. When the snowball missed the target completely, Julian gave a war cry and ran at Lionel to knock him to the ground. There he smashed a soft snowball into Lionel's face, drenching him thoroughly.

Lionel grunted. His brother was as bulky as a bear, and twice as persistent.

"Cry peace!" Julian demanded.

"Peace!" Lionel echoed dutifully. Julian hauled him to his feet and ran off at young Matthew's laughing summons, so Lionel brushed himself off, fashioned a new missile and looked about eagerly for a fresh victim.

Something else he had missed during his years of living from hand-to-mouth in the city was the exhilaration of a good snowball fight.

"Save me!" cried a laughing Mary Ann, running around a tree with her nephews and the dog in pursuit.

She ran right into Lionel's arms, and he held her close for a moment as they were pelted with snowballs at knee level and the boys screamed with glee at Mary Ann's spirited cries of dismay.

"Are you cold?" he asked, looking down into Mary Ann's laughing eyes when the boys and the dog ran off to joyfully circle Matthew and Julian. She was trembling in her snow-encrusted burgundy pelisse.

Her smile faded.

"Not anymore," she said gravely as she snuggled more closely into his arms.

He curled one finger around a damp ringlet. Her hair was hanging in soggy strings, her nose was red and never had she looked so beautiful to him.

"My mother is going to kill me for getting my hair all wet before the ball," she said with an impish smile. "It will have to be washed and curled again."

"Why?" he teased. "I think it looks very fetching like this."

She was irresistible. He bent to taste her pretty, cherry-red lips, but Mary Ann laid a hand against his chest to prevent him.

"Lionel," Mary Ann whispered with regret in her eyes. "We are in plain sight of the parlor window."

"So we are," he replied huskily as he drew her into the cover of a nearby clump of trees and bushes.

"Well, Garland," said Lionel when he finished tying his cravat with a precision that he hadn't lost in his years of exile from society. "Will I do?"

"Splendidly, sir," the valet said with a proud smile as he handed Lionel his gloves. Like any good valet, Garland had stood at attention—afraid even to breathe—while his master completed the intricate task of arranging the snowy neckcloth just so. Amazing how Garland had once again picked up the rhythm and graces of serving in a grand house. "Miss Whittaker will be quite smitten, if you will permit me to say so."

"Garland," Lionel said in reproachful accents. Who would have thought his pragmatic manservant was a secret romantic?

"The young lady does seem to favor you, sir," Garland said with a twinkle in his eyes. "It would not be unheard of for an advantageous match to be made at a Christmas ball."

"Advantageous, is it?" Lionel exclaimed. "Not for *her*, surely. Lord Blakely would show us the door instantly if I had the everlasting cheek to offer for the girl, so I'll thank you not to noise that bit of whimsy below stairs."

"As you wish, sir," Garland said. But the maddeningly confident smile did not leave his face.

The manservant had brushed Lionel's best—and only—evening dress coat with reverent fingers and polished Lionel's soft leather dancing slippers until they were positively shining. He was hovering over Lionel just like a fond mama preparing her daughter for a ball.

On that repulsive thought, Lionel bade Garland not to wait up for him and strolled down to the drawing room, which was occupied by the gentlemen of the household, the Langtry children and Amy and Aggie.

The ladies, of course, would make an entrance later. The gentlemen would all stand to attention when they did so, and bow as if they were in the presence of a flock of royal princesses instead of their own wives and sisters.

Lionel surprised himself by smiling in anticipation. He had grown to enjoy the elegant folly of a fashionable gentleman's house. He would miss all of this splendor almost as much as Garland would.

Surprisingly, Lionel's father was the only one who looked at daggers drawn when he came into the room, although neither the Earl of Stoneham nor Lord Renfield acknowledged his presence in any way.

Lord Blakely greeted Lionel civilly, as did Julian, who braved a scowl from his father to do so. Robert Langtry favored Lionel with a firm handshake and complimented him upon his impeccable aim at snowball throwing.

Mary Ann and Melissa no doubt had been forced to endure the hysterical scolding of their mothers and their maids for participating in a raucous snowball fight with the children and returning to the house in a sadly bedraggled state a mere two hours before dinner. They would keep the gentlemen waiting until well past the appointed hour.

Lionel had been enchanted by the sight of Mary Ann with her hair in sodden ringlets and her eyes sparkling as she and her shrieking twin nephews chased each other all over the yard. Unlike most ladies of his acquaintance, she genuinely enjoyed the company of children and would not hold her own at arm's length when the time came for her to have them.

Careful, old fellow. You are not going to be anywhere near the lady when that happens.

Lionel didn't dare let Mary Ann's fervent kisses go to his head. He had been a fool to respond to that glowing look in her eyes because she was like fine wine: One intoxicating sip, and a man wouldn't be able to stop himself from drinking it dry.

Blakely might be grateful to Lionel for saving him from discovery as the object of Lady Cavenish's most lascivious desires, but that didn't mean he had any intention of welcoming Lionel into the family.

Barbara took another drink of the brandy she had spirited away from Lord Blakely's library and been nursing all day in the privacy of her boudoir, where she had retreated just after breakfast pleading one of her headaches, according to her sister's instructions.

Beatrice insisted she could not trust Barbara not to embarrass them all and ruin her precious Julian's chances of making a good impression on Lord Blakely. She had been quite unpleasant about it.

This unfair treatment from her sister rankled and festered like a canker.

Barbara was a marchioness, was she not? She knew perfectly well how to behave in company *far* more splendid than any to be found in *Leicestershire,* of all places. Princes and diplomats and grand dukes all paid homage to her beauty in ways that Beatrice could only *dream* of.

Yet here she was, bullied by her forceful sister into staying in her boudoir all evening with nothing but her own thoughts to keep her company. She might have derived some satisfaction from bullying her maid, but the girl made Barbara so cross with her fussing and gossiping that Barbara had told the clumsy chit to get out of her sight and take that yappy, disgusting lapdog with her!

Beatrice already had made excuses on Barbara's behalf to their hostess, claiming that Barbara was far too overset by her ordeal at Lionel's hands to attend the ball.

To add insult to injury, Barbara's window had given her a clear view of the grounds below, where a spirited snowball fight was in progress.

The rancor in her heart fed on the sight of Lionel and that cow-eyed girl laughing and playing in the snow below.

Barbara was willing to wager her next quarter-day pin money that neither realized an excellent view of their trysting place behind some convenient trees was perfectly accessible from Barbara's upstairs window.

Trust Lionel merely to rain chaste, fervent kisses on the girl's enraptured face instead of taking advantage of the situation for greater liberties. It was plain from the girl's demeanor that *she* would make no protest.

Barbara burned with jealousy and self-pity, but she couldn't look away.

Lionel kissed the girl on the eyelids. Then he enfolded her in his strong arms and held her to his chest as if he would never let her go.

Barbara's heart pounded.

He used to kiss *her* that way!

Even though Lionel didn't disarrange an inch of Miss Whittaker's clothing or touch her anywhere that he shouldn't, their passion for each other practically melted the snow from the trees.

Was Barbara so old that no one would ever love her in that way again?

No!

He would love her.

He *must* love her.

She would make him so mad with passion that he would have no choice but to love her.

Emboldened by the brandy, her brain hatched an audacious plan that would show the object of her adoration how useless it was for him to think he could escape her.

And her triumph would put her manipulative sister in her place once and for all!

It cost a pang to give up the satisfaction of stunning all the gentlemen in the delicious ballgown of sea green gauze and silver tissue made for her by a leading *modiste* in Paris, but there would be other balls.

After all, there was only one gentleman at this boring party she wished to impress, and before the night was over, he would be hers.

A little flurry of activity at the entrance to the drawing room announced the arrival of the ladies, with Lady

Letitia and Lady Madelyn, both earl's daughters and therefore first in consequence, in the lead. They were positively dripping in diamonds and emeralds, respectively, but it was Mary Ann who captured Lionel's complete attention.

She was wearing a simple ivory gown that shimmered subtly with crystal beads. Her glossy dark hair was arranged high on her head and secured with ivory roses, as it had been the first time he saw her. Her only jewelry was a gold chain at her throat and a pair of pearl teardrop earrings.

"Here's our snow maiden," he said, smiling, when she approached him.

"And she will be fortunate if she does not catch a chill," her loving mother said with grim foreboding.

"Yes, Mother," Mary Ann said with deceptive meekness.

Lady St. James gave her son an unsubtle jab in his ribs.

"Uh, Miss Whittaker," Julian said, jerking forward as if pulled by invisible strings. "May I escort you to dinner?"

Mary Ann smiled and placed her hand on Julian's extended arm with every appearance of pleasure.

For her to do otherwise, Lionel told himself, would have been a grave breach of etiquette.

He firmly checked a ridiculous impulse to seize Mary Ann's other arm and treat the assembled company to the shocking spectacle of a tug-of-war.

Instead, he bowed to the two Whittaker misses not yet out when he saw all the older ladies had been paired off with appropriate gentlemen.

"Miss Amy, Miss Agatha," he observed. "I perceive you have no escort into dinner. May I?"

"Oh, *thank* you, Mr. St. James," the thrilled girls breathed in chorus as they each accepted one of his arms.

Lionel was rewarded by a radiant look from Mary Ann and a sour one from his stepmother as the glittering procession entered the dining room.

Fifteen

The stupid slut would ruin everything!

How could Lord Renfield have known Lady Cavenish would follow him here after their brief, satisfactory liaison? It had amused him to play the ardent lover when their paths crossed months ago in Paris.

He had been traveling alone, and she had been staying at a hotel with her inattentive husband. She flirted with him at a very dull party. He flirted back, flattered that such a charming and much sought-after, if somewhat older, lady found him to her taste. It was inevitable that they would relieve their respective boredom together in such a romantic city.

When it was time for him to return to London, they parted with mutual expressions of passion, and he had assumed that hers were no more serious than his. For his part, the affair was an exciting change of pace from the banality of his oppressively respectable life, for a man with high ambitions in politics did not dare let the whisper of scandal attach to his name in his own city.

Now, back in England and refreshed by his tempestuous affair with the beautiful noblewoman, he was shocked when Lady Cavenish appeared in Leicestershire pledging her undying devotion and determined to leave her husband to run away to the Continent with him! He did recall getting carried away by his own ardor and making such a proposal in those last, mad days before his ship was to sail, but it never occurred to him that a woman of such obvious sophistication would take him seriously.

She apparently had found out from the society pages that he was to attend Lord Blakely's house party. He had trusted his failure to respond to her summons to a tryst in Lord Blakely's library last evening would suffice to discourage her from further unwelcome attentions, but apparently he had been mistaken.

The lady's charms were not inconsiderable, but hardly enough to tempt him to ruin what would be a brilliant career and risk being plunged into disgrace. He had been at such great pains to cultivate an image of incorruptible honesty and integrity in public, only to have *this* happen.

Fury made his jaw clench and his fists knot when she came tripping into the candy-box salon that she had designated in her coyly phrased missive for their rendezvous. His anger rose when he recalled the bold look the creature's maid had given him as she handed him the note. He thought about ignoring Lady Cavenish's summons, but he knew she would only find other—and possibly less discreet—ways of getting him alone.

He had to put an end to this dangerous folly at once!

"Lucas, darling. I knew you would not fail me," Lady Cavenish said, smiling triumphantly at him. She was very sure of her powers. Her voluptuous body was clad in a low-cut white gown, and diamonds glittered at her ears and throat. Her hair was undressed and flowed over her lovely white shoulders.

She undulated across the room and placed one soft, pampered hand against his cheek.

He supposed this was his cue to sweep her into his arms and devour her face with his kisses, or some such Fustian rubbish, he thought resentfully. Instead, he turned his face away from her questing lips.

To his annoyance, she gave a coquettish little giggle.

"Don't pout, darling. I know it was naughty of me to come here, but are you not a little happy to see me?"

"No, Lady Cavenish," he said stiffly, "I am not. I think I made it clear to you at our last meeting on the Continent that our affair was at an end."

Her frown caused her facial muscles to sag. He suspected she would never frown again if she knew how old and stupid it made her look.

"You said that if I were free, you would run away with me to the Continent."

"I said *if* you were free. Good God, woman! You are married, and you have three children."

"I am leaving my husband. I told you that."

"You may commit any folly you choose," he grated out as he removed her clinging hands from where she had flung them around his neck. "It is nothing to me."

When he pushed her away, she reached out one trembling hand toward him. Her quivering lips formed his name as she sank gracefully to her knees in supplication.

It needed only that! She disgusted him utterly.

He turned away from her to make good his escape, but she sprang forward and wrapped both her arms around his legs. She even allowed herself to be dragged a short distance when he started walking.

"Do get a grip on yourself, madam!" he said coldly as he kicked out at her to free himself.

It was an accident. He *swore* to himself it was an accident.

But his shoe smashed into her face and she cried out.

"Look what you have done to me!" she cried as the blood stained her nose and dripped onto the white bosom of her dress. It really was quite a lot of blood. He was rather fascinated by the sight of it.

"It is your own fault for provoking me," Renfield said.

She jumped up and ran at him with her claws extended and her teeth bared. She looked like a harpy at full attack.

"Monster!" she cried out as she drew one hand back to slap him.

She must not mark his face! It was his only thought.

So he drew back his fist and hit her before she could do so.

Dazed, she landed on the floor in a heap of crumpled white fabric. Her eyes were wide and tears ran down her cheeks to mingle with the blood smearing her face. This sight both aroused and disgusted him.

"Monster," she cried out again. "I hate you! I will tell my sister. I will tell the *world*."

He laughed at her. He couldn't help himself. It had felt *good* to wipe the smug look off her face with his fist.

"I shouldn't, if I were you, my sweet," he drawled. "For one thing, who would believe your word against mine? My reputation is quite beyond reproach, which is more than I can say for yours."

"I despise you," she whispered vehemently.

His answer was another heartless laugh. The feeling was entirely mutual.

"If you are wise, you will keep to your room for the next few days," he advised her. "You can always tell your affectionate sister that you fell down the stairs."

"I will see you dishonored. I swear I will."

He bent down and pinched her chin cruelly as he forced her to raise her battered face to his.

"Oh, I think not, my sweet," he said softly. He could smell her fear. "Or I will see you *dead*." He smiled sardonically as he echoed her own words. "I swear I will."

To his satisfaction, she inched away from him and cowered against the wall. She believed him at last.

With a light heart, he returned to the dancing. It wouldn't do for his absence to occasion remark.

* * *

Mrs. Whittaker glowed with satisfaction as Lord Renfield led Mary Ann in the steps of the quadrille.

"Do they not make a charming couple?" she said to Lionel, who was standing nearby, torturing himself by watching Mary Ann smile into the handsome young man's face. All the ladies adored the good-looking viscount, damn his eyes! His own sister went into a bemused trance at the mere sound of his name.

"Charming," Lionel echoed dutifully, acknowledging reluctantly that they did, indeed, look well together. Renfield had dark hair and darker eyes. His birth was good. His fortune was better. And never had the breath of scandal been associated with his name. No doubt Lord Blakely would be thrilled to welcome *him* to the family.

When Renfield had entered the room just now, Lord Blakely placed a casual arm over his shoulders, and Lionel's breast burned with an emotion that was perilously akin to jealousy.

That was when he realized he not only was enamored of Mary Ann, but also of her affectionate family. Even *Blakely,* for heaven's sake, despite the fact that he merely tolerated Lionel's presence in his house and was willing to pay handsomely to be rid of him at the appointed time.

Well, what else had Lionel expected?

The truth was, Renfield was the answer to a maiden's prayer. Why should Mary Ann alone be immune to his obvious attractions?

The consummate politician, Renfield had shared his favors politely and impartially with every young lady in the room and been gallant toward the older ones. But he held Mary Ann a little closer than he had the others when he danced with her. And his dark head was bent to hers often to share confidences. He made her *laugh,* damn his eyes!

"Well, Lionel," said Melissa, slipping her gloved hand

into his. "Will you not dance the next set with your sister, or would you prefer to prop up the wall all night?"

"With pleasure," he said at once. "If your mother will not step between us."

Melissa made a moue of annoyance.

"Oh, *Mother,*" she said, rolling her eyes. "Try to pay her no heed. I never do."

Lionel burst out laughing.

Melissa had always been a bit of a rebel, bless her. It pleased him that her domineering mother had not succeeded in squelching her vibrant spirit.

"And if you could contrive to steer us, ever so subtly, in Lord Renfield's direction when we are finished dancing . . ." she suggested coyly.

"See here, Melissa," he snapped. *"You* are not interested in that popinjay, are you?"

The girl's eyes grew round.

"You sounded just like Papa!" she exclaimed. "Lionel! Are you feeling quite the thing?"

"I don't know what came over me," he said, just as shocked as she was by his outburst.

"Well, never mind," she said as she watched Renfield flirt with Mary Ann. "It's plain the man prefers brunettes."

Lionel touched Melissa's golden curls.

"There is no accounting for taste, after all," he said soothingly. Melissa looked very pretty dressed all in white with festive red ribbons in her hair. The affectionate little girl he remembered so fondly had turned into a diamond of the first water, and he had not been around to see this stunning transformation.

The thought made him sad.

"Come along, love," he said to his sister as the dance ended and the next set formed. He made no resistance when the little minx led them right into the same set as Mary Ann and Renfield. It was a country dance, and, if he knew his little sister, she would manage affairs so that Renfield would be compelled by good manners to partner her for the next set when the dance ended.

Lionel had mixed feelings about this. Melissa's maneuver would make it easy for him to claim Mary Ann for the next dance unless she was promised to another man. But he did not like the thought of Renfield trifling with Melissa any more than he liked the idea of Renfield trifling with Mary Ann.

Melissa's dowry had to be a significant one, and even the most objective observer had to acknowledge her considerable personal attractions. But Renfield could look much higher among the Upper Ten Thousand for a bride, and if the blackguard broke his little sister's heart, Lionel would make him very, very sorry.

Lionel took a deep, calming breath. He was jumping to conclusions, of course. He hardly knew the man, after all. His dislike for Renfield no doubt stemmed from jealousy because of his attentions to Mary Ann. That, and the fact that Renfield was everything Lionel was not.

As if his emotions weren't tumultuous enough, a fourth couple joined their set—his father and stepmother. Now, what could *they* be about? They were the oldest couple on the floor, and neither was smiling. Of course, it could be no more than his stepmother's desire to climb the social ladder—they had joined the set right after Lady Madelyn and her husband approached.

Such a civilized little family group, he thought sourly.

He bowed mechanically to his sister in the opening steps of the country dance as the music began; then the ladies formed an inner circle and after several revolutions dropped back from their original positions to face the next gentleman in line.

Mary Ann, his new partner, pretended to cower back in trepidation.

"Good heavens, Mr. St. James! If you could see your face!"

Despite the disturbing presence of his father and stepmother in the set, Lionel's mood magically lightened as he smiled down into the eyes of the woman he adored.

"I know exactly what you are thinking," she said as he put his arm around her waist and promenaded with her around the circle of dancers. "There is something about Lord Renfield that one cannot quite like."

"You seemed to like him perfectly well a moment ago," Lionel said. It was good to know that Mary Ann wasn't taken in by Renfield's pretty face and pretty manners.

"I was being polite. Mama would have the vapors if I refused to dance with such an eligible gentleman, but I find him conceited beyond permission. Arrogant, too, for I was promised this dance to your brother, and Renfield cut him off quite rudely when he attempted to claim me. I would have refused to dance with him again if it wouldn't have made a dreadful scene."

Lionel was so busy digesting this that Mary Ann had to struggle to release her hands from his tightened grip.

"Time to change partners," she said gaily when she managed to extricate herself.

Lionel bowed to Lady Madelyn, his next temporary partner.

"Lovely ball," she said politely.

"Yes. Lovely," he agreed.

The very rich, very socially prominent earl's daughter took no offense to his obvious inattention. To Lionel's chagrin, a knowing smile touched her lips and brightened her green eyes.

"Miss Whittaker looks very beautiful tonight, does she not?" she asked.

"She always does," he said solemnly.

"And your sister, too, of course. Such a sweet, pretty-behaved girl."

"Thank you," Lionel said, gratified by this praise of Melissa. He appreciated the kindness that prompted Lady Madelyn to converse with him as if he, too, were connected to a family. And, more importantly, she behaved as if he had a perfect right to admire Mary Ann if he chose to do so. Lady Madelyn must know that he was in disgrace and hardly a desirable acquaintance for a gently bred virgin. For a moment he almost felt as if he belonged here.

There were those who styled Lady Madelyn a snob, but Lionel would never be one of their number.

With a smile, he released her to join her next partner.

Then he cringed, for the next woman to spin into his arms was his stepmother.

"Lionel," she said coldly. Her lips were smiling, but her eyes were hard.

"Lady St. James," he said, just as coldly. They managed to touch with just the tips of their gloved fingers. He waited to see if she would broach the matter that had caused her to herd his father into the set.

"I believe the best thing for all of us would be for you to leave this house quietly. Will you do that for the sake of simple decency?"

He had to give her the plum. She got right to the point.

"No, Lady St. James, I will not," he said pleasantly. "I am promised to Lord and Lady Blakely until the New Year." At which point he would be unceremoniously shown the door, but he'd be dashed if he told *her* that.

She gave him a forbidding frown, but Lionel was impervious to her black looks. He had been favored with far too many of them to be affected by them now.

"Lord Renfield has been showing a definite interest in Melissa, and Julian is in a fair way of becoming engaged to the Whittaker girl."

Lionel gave her a look of disbelief. Was she *blind?* Any interest she imagined on Renfield's part for Melissa or

Mary Ann's for Julian was nothing but wishful thinking on the part of an ambitious matchmaking mother.

He hoped.

"There is a saying about chickens," he said vaguely. "Counting them or something."

"It is of the utmost importance that we make a good impression on Lord Blakely and his family. I know you have always detested me, but you seem to have some tepid affection for Melissa and Julian. Do not ruin their chances of happiness."

"How very strange this sounds, coming from you, madam," he said quietly. "I have not known you to be very much concerned with anyone's happiness except your own."

Her jaw hardened.

"I should have known better than to appeal to *your* sense of decency."

"Yes," he agreed, unscrupulously goading her when he knew Lady Madelyn's presence in the same set would prohibit her from ringing a peal over his unrepentant head. "You should."

Fortunately for both of them, perhaps, the movement of the dance compelled her to drop back into the next gentleman's arms, while Melissa danced into Lionel's.

"How goes the hunt, minx?" he asked, amused by her melting look of farewell at Renfield when she exchanged him for her brother.

She gave a dramatic sigh, and for a moment Lionel was reminded unpleasantly of her aunt, Lady Cavenish.

But only for a moment.

Melissa was possessed of a lively sense of humor that mitigated the effect of her airs.

He grinned and gave her a brotherly little shove when she rolled her eyes expressively and started fanning herself with her gloved hand.

"Well enough, I suppose," she said brightly. "At the

risk of being vulgar, my dowry is *much* larger than Mary Ann's. And, of course, I *am* a blonde." She batted her eyes at him.

"There is that, of course. But, my dear, you can do much better than him."

"How very touching!" she said affectionately. "But your fondness blinds your eyes." She licked her lips, again reminding him of Barbara. "It would be rather difficult to do better than *that!*" She gave a languid wave of her hand toward Renfield, who was looming over Mary Ann with so much attentive gallantry that Lionel longed to throw the circle into chaos by planting him a facer. Melissa sighed again.

At that moment, the dancers faced the center of the circle with linked hands, and Lionel saw his father—who was once again partnering his wife—staring at him.

Lionel stared back, so it was impossible to ignore the jerk of his father's head toward the door of the ballroom.

Reluctantly, Lionel nodded.

The old man wanted to talk to him for the first time in ten years, but Lionel didn't delude himself that this conversation would be any more pleasant than their last one.

To his annoyance, his stepmother smiled complacently as Renfield asked a delighted Melissa to dance. Her cup ran over when Lady Madelyn addressed a polite comment to her, and Mary Ann approached Julian to make amends, no doubt, for Renfield's appropriation of Julian's dance with her.

Lionel's father clapped him on the shoulder.

"Come along," he said forbiddingly. "It is time we had a talk."

The boy refused to sit, even when Sir Andrew gestured toward the seat opposite Lord Blakely's desk.

Stiff-rumped as always.

The baronet sighed.

"Your stepmother and I want you to leave this place," he began.

"No," Lionel said pleasantly. "Was there anything else?"

"Burn it, Lionel! You have already caused talk with whatever transpired between you and Barbara. Your presence here is an embarrassment."

"I understand that," the familiar, yet unfamiliar, voice continued reasonably. "But I am remaining, just the same."

Sir Andrew was thrown off stride. It was once so easy to draw Lionel into an impassioned argument, to poke holes through his reasoning, to bully him into grudging compliance.

But something happened that Sir Andrew had not anticipated when he threw his son out of his house—he had learned restraint. He had learned to focus on the subject at hand instead of allowing himself to be sidetracked into minor issues.

Lionel had become a man, and his father had not been there to see it. Now his firstborn was a complete stranger.

A wave of sadness swept over the older man in mourning for those ten lost years.

That bright, passionate boy of whom he had been so proud was gone, and in his place was this cold stranger, this rapscallion who made his living from fleecing the gullible at cards.

Lionel's face gave away nothing as he returned his father's most intimidating glare.

Sir Andrew might have been staring at a total stranger as, indeed, he was.

He knew that to break eye contact or to speak would be to give his estranged son the advantage.

To Perdition with advantage!

"Have you been . . . well, Lionel?"

The familiar, yet unfamiliar, man frowned.

"Have I been . . . well?" he repeated, as if it was the last question he expected his father to ask.

"Yes, deuce take it!" Sir Andrew said in exasperation. "It is a simple question, Lionel."

"I know. I am simply surprised. Yes, I suppose you could say I am well."

He paused and gave a self-conscious smile.

"Thank you for asking."

Sir Andrew blinked rapidly. In that moment he saw a glimpse of his son's old sweetness. He had seen it off and on the past few days as Lionel conversed with members of Lady Blakely's family and even his own half brother and sister. Sir Andrew just never expected to see it directed toward himself again.

"And you . . . Father?" Lionel's voice cracked a little on the word. "Have you been well? Truly?"

Sir Andrew almost told the truth—that the past ten years had been pure hell as he watched his younger children grow up and mourned the son who was missing.

That a part of *himself* had been missing.

"Capital," he lied instead. "Never better."

"Well, then," Lionel said, allowing that impassive mask to slip over his face again. "If you will excuse me?"

Sir Andrew gave his son a dismissive wave of his hand, knowing the moment was lost.

Lionel bowed and was gone.

Sixteen

Julian gave a long sigh as Mary Ann kept twisting around in his arms to get a clear view of the doorway. It made the waltz more dizzying than usual.

"If I promise to tell you the moment he appears, will you stop *doing* that?" he asked plaintively. "I feel like I'm dancing with a buttered eel."

"I'm so sorry," said Mary Ann, conscience-stricken, as she smiled ruefully into her partner's exasperated face. Lionel and his father had been gone for an age, and she so hoped they had mended their differences.

"I can see my mother is the only one who thinks I'm the answer to a maiden's prayer."

"Your *mother,*" Mary Ann began with some heat. The way the woman had snubbed Lionel at every opportunity had done nothing to endear her to Mary Ann. Then she broke off and bit her lip. Lady St. James might be a horror, but she was Julian's mother, and he gave every indication of being a dutiful son.

"Quite," Julian said with so much vehemence that Mary Ann burst out laughing.

Then she saw Lionel come into the room, and the laughter died. His face was very, very grave. Not a good sign.

Julian gave a stifled shout of pain.

"That was my *foot,* Miss Whittaker!" he complained. "If you do not wish to dance, you have only to say so. It is quite unnecessary to cripple me."

"I beg your pardon, Mr. St. James," she said at once, but her voice sounded distracted even to her own ears. Julian sighed again.

"I take it my prodigal brother has returned to the ballroom," he said with a sigh, "and you are wishing me to Jericho."

"Of course not," she said, forcing herself to smile at Julian instead of craning her neck to see what Lionel was doing.

"Miss Whittaker. If you should someday find yourself up River Tick, do not, I beg of you, seek to recoup your fortunes on the stage. You would starve within the week."

He meant it to sound playful, but it rang false.

"Ah. He and Melissa are together," Julian continued as he deliberately steered his partner in that direction. "That makes things simpler."

"I am so sorry," she said, sensing his disappointment.

He didn't pretend to misunderstand her.

"Not at all. My mother will get over it, and so shall I. You are the first young lady she has ever completely approved of for me. This gives me hope there are more . . . somewhere."

"I do like you so much," she said, feeling awful. "You are so good-natured."

"Please. Say nothing more. We can't have your faint praise going to my head," he replied wryly. "Here you go, Lionel. Dance with the chit, and mind your toes," he said, contriving to arrive before Lionel and Melissa as the music ended. "Come along, Melissa. I'm of a mind to do my brotherly duty."

Renfield had almost reached them, but he stopped in his tracks when Julian started to escort his sister to the dance floor.

Julian rolled his eyes heavenward.

"Renfield, have you *no* imagination? I have only to

claim a partner and you must decide you want her for yourself."

"Julian," Melissa said, showing him her dance card. "I *am* promised to Lord Renfield for this dance."

"Yes, and we all know *that* is Holy Writ!" he said sarcastically as he favored that gentleman with an acid look. "Never mind. I am not such a slowtop that I am obliged to dance with my own sister for want of a partner." He gave Melissa's pert nose a brotherly tweak, bowed to the ladies and sauntered off with his dignity intact.

Mary Ann almost applauded.

With stars in her eyes, Melissa laid her hand on Renfield's arm and prepared to go with him to the next set.

"May I have the set after this, Miss Whittaker?" Renfield asked.

"We have already danced twice, Lord Renfield," she reminded him. Mrs. Whittaker persisted in deluding herself that Mary Ann might reconsider her refusal of Lord Renfield's flattering offer, but pigs would fly first! "To do so again would occasion remark."

The urbane smile hardened on Renfield's face.

"As you wish," Renfield said after a moment. He turned from her to smile down at his partner, and Mary Ann could almost hear Melissa's heart flutter. "Miss St. James?"

The couple had not taken three steps before Melissa's bubbling laughter rang out and she rapped Renfield's shoulder playfully with her fan. Mary Ann supposed he had said something amusing—and probably derogatory—about her.

She didn't care. Her only concern now was Lionel.

"We needn't dance if you would rather not," she said tentatively. "I can tell by the look on your face that it didn't go well."

He smiled at her.

"It went as well as I could have expected. He asked me

to leave this house; I refused. But it didn't end in the two of us shouting at one another. One might call that progress of a sort."

Mary Ann held him back when he would have led her onto the dance floor.

"Another country dance," she said. "I would rather not. Come with me."

She took his arm and practically dragged him out of the ballroom, down the stairs and into one of the small salons on the ground floor. The room was cast in semi-darkness, with only a candle or two lit on low tables. Like every other room in the house, it was decorated with greenery, and Mary Ann could smell the pine boughs before her eyes had adjusted to the shadows well enough for her to see them. Once inside the room and away from prying eyes, she took both of Lionel's hands and placed them around her own waist. Then she rose up on her toes to put her arms around his neck and give him a hug.

Somehow Mary Ann knew how his conversation with his father had disappointed him. Against all reason, he had hoped . . . for what? He wasn't even sure *what* he had hoped for.

But he forgot all about his father when Mary Ann raised her lips to his and, heaven help him, he had to fight to control a hunger that had been building since that first evening in Lord Stoneham's ballroom, when she looked at him as if he were Sir Galahad returned to Camelot with the Holy Grail.

"Miss Whittaker," he breathed. "This is wrong. We must not—"

Despite his protests, his hands almost of their own volition framed her face.

"This is *right*," she said softly. "How can you deny it is right for us to be together after this afternoon?"

He could have told her that the kisses they exchanged in the snow meant nothing to him. That kissing pretty girls was one of the delights of the season, like searching for the ring in the plum pudding or drinking spiced wine. But he could not pretend with her.

"That was a mistake," he said, even as he crushed her tightly in his arms and planted kisses at the corner of her mouth, her temple and even on her nose between words. *"This* is a mistake."

He took her lips in a kiss that shook them both.

"Lionel," she sighed when they had to break apart so they could breathe. Then she frowned and put a hand to his chest to prevent him from kissing her again. "Did you hear that?"

At first he resisted, but he released her when he saw her head was turned away from him and cocked to one side.

Then he heard it, too—a faint animal keening that gave him chills as it rose on a mournful note.

They had been so intent on each other that they hadn't seen her cowering in a dark corner near the fireplace. The light from the candles on the mantel made her eyes look empty in their sunken sockets. In her crushed white dress and with her pale hair leeched to frost in the dim candle-light, the only color about her was the spatter of drying blood on her face and the front of her dress. Then she looked up at them, and her eyes showed white all around their blue irises.

"Barbara," Lionel said softly as he knelt before her. "Who has done this to you?"

She gave a faint moan and cowered back.

"Here, my dear," he said with a gentleness that brought tears to Mary Ann's eyes and made her ashamed of the many times she had wished Lady Cavenish and her arts and graces to Perdition. The poor lady was not pretending now. "Let me help you."

Lady Cavenish shrank back from him with fear on her face.

"You cannot stay here on the cold floor," he continued kindly and reasonably. So had Mary Ann's now-dead father talked to his children in those distant days before drink had consumed his life. "Come now, there's a good girl," he said as Lady Cavenish gave a little cry of surrender and put her trembling hand in his.

"That's right," he said soothingly as he carefully put his arms around the woman and stood up with her cradled protectively in his arms. "That's a brave girl."

"I will fetch your sister and your maid," Mary Ann said reassuringly to Lady Cavenish.

"No! You must not!" she cried in agitation. "Not Beatrice!"

"Just your maid, then," Mary Ann said at once. "And we must tell Alexander. Whoever has done this to you must be found."

"No! No! You must not tell Lord Blakely or *anyone!*" she cried. "He will kill me if you do."

Mary Ann and Lionel exchanged startled looks.

But before they could question her further, the poor lady fainted.

"You *cannot* think it is true," Mary Ann said adamantly after Lionel had carried Lady Cavenish to her bedchamber and left her in the care of her maid. "Alexander could *not* be responsible for her condition."

"I do not know *what* to think," he admitted.

"Only a monster could have done such a thing."

"Or a man who is desperate to keep his life from crumbling all about him," he said softly.

There was pity in his eyes. *Pity! For her!*

Well, Mary Ann would have none of it!

She grasped his coat by the lapels and pulled him down to her level so his face was within inches of hers.

"Take that look off your face, Lionel St. James!" she demanded. "She is distraught! She does not know what she is saying! It was someone else. An intruder."

"It is as you say, of course," he said in that kind tone of voice he had used with Lady Cavenish as he surrounded Mary Ann's cold fingers with his warm, gentle hands.

It made her absolutely furious!

"Alexander did *not* do it," she insisted as she pulled her hands out of his.

"Of course not," he said bitterly. "It is so much easier to sacrifice an outsider when the evidence conflicts with what we wish to believe of someone we hold in high esteem. My God, Mary Ann. Is no one interested in the *truth?* No doubt a scapegoat will be found, and I pity the poor devil, for it will not matter to any of you whether he is innocent or guilty as long as your precious brother-in-law's reputation is protected."

Mary Ann's eyes narrowed at this outburst.

"That's what happened to you, isn't it?" It was a statement, not a question. "They sacrificed your reputation for hers. I *knew* it!"

He turned his back on her.

"I have no idea what you are talking about."

"You never abducted her at all," she said, walking around to face him.

His silence confirmed her words.

"I think you had better tell me the whole story," she said.

"We cannot talk here," he said.

"We will go somewhere else, then," she snapped as she seized his wrist and towed him off down the hall.

"Good God," Lionel said, looking as if he had been ushered to a dungeon complete with rack and iron maiden instead of a perfectly ordinary lady's bedchamber. "We cannot stay *here!* What if someone discovers us?"

"My reputation would be in shreds," Mary Ann told him matter-of-factly. "The sooner you make a clean breast of it, the sooner you can escape to the safety of the ball-room. Now. Tell me the truth—did you abduct your step-mother's sister and force her to elope with you to Gretna Green?"

Lionel gave a snort of derision.

"My dear girl, I understand your skepticism," he said, brushing an infinitesimal mote of dust from his dark coat. "It *is* rather fatiguing to bear off a desperately struggling female, but I was ten years younger, you know, and the lady herself was rather less . . . abundant than she is now."

"Do *not* make the very grave error of patronizing me, Lionel," Mary Ann said in a dangerously calm voice. "Answer the question. *Did* you abduct her?"

He gave a muttered curse and threw his hands up in capitulation.

"Very well, if you *must* know!" he said with a bitter laugh. "It was all *her* idea. She *begged* me to carry her off to Gretna Green to save her from the marriage her sister and my father had arranged for her with the marquess, and I, conceited young fool that I was, was suffering from such a pitiful case of calf love for the lady that I was eager to agree. It was all very romantic and exciting until my father and her fiancé caught up with us on the road to Scotland. I actually drew a pistol on my own father to defend the poor, persecuted darling from the cruel men who would force her into a loveless marriage."

He shook his head. "What an idiot I was."

"Go on," she prompted. "What happened next?"

He gave her a smile that did not reach his eyes.

"Well, you may imagine my consternation when she threw herself upon my father's bosom and thanked him for her deliverance from a fate worse than death," he said in a valiant attempt to make an amusing story of it. "Before I could get a word in edgewise, she swooned grace-fully into the marquess's arthritic arms. Quite the drama queen, was Barbara. She decided she'd rather be a marchioness, after all, and so she claimed I abducted her against her will."

"And your father *believed* this Banbury tale?" Mary Ann exclaimed indignantly.

Lionel surprised her very much by giving her a quick kiss on the lips.

"Thank you for the vote of confidence, love. My father *wanted* to believe it, which amounts to the same thing. Barbara's marriage to the marquess would elevate us in the standing of the world. *Nothing* must be allowed to interfere with that."

"You might have told your father the truth."

"Oh, my dear girl, what would have been the use?" Lionel said with a bitter travesty of a smile at her naïveté. "He was much more interested in placating his hysterical wife and protecting her sister from scandal than he was in hearing the truth from me, I assure you. He was still besotted with her then. And, of course, *she* had conveniently provided him with a spare heir for whom she was anxious to secure my father's fortune. It was expedient— for the sake of the family honor, you understand—to sacrifice me to absolve Barbara from blame. I was already accounted to be very wild; my father and stepmother encouraged the marquess to believe his blushing bride's pretty story so he would still marry her."

"So your father disinherited you."

Mary Ann looked so distressed that Lionel longed to kiss her again, but he managed with some difficulty to restrain himself. It had been a long time since anyone had believed in him so completely.

"Oh, no. He didn't disinherit me *then*," he said bitterly. "He made arrangements to send me away for a few months. Wonderful thing, how efficient people can be when they want to rid themselves of someone who has become an embarrassment. In my absence, Barbara and the marquess would marry as planned. Eventually, when the whole thing had blown over, I could return to the bosom of my family to assume my rightful place as his heir."

"And you refused to obey him," Mary Ann said.

"Yes," he said wryly. "Instead, I left his house and took lodgings in London. The marriage went off as planned, and my father invented a convenient illness to explain my absence. But the tale that painted Barbara as an unwilling victim of my unbridled lusts was all over London practically before the wedding cake was distributed to the guests."

"How could *anyone* have accepted such a ridiculous story!"

"The marquess certainly accepted it. He challenged me to a duel as a sop to his own pride once the story got about."

"Did you meet him?"

"Certainly not!" Lionel snapped. "He was thirty years my senior! What a figure I should cut!"

"Refusing to meet him was the same as a public admission of guilt. Even I know that!"

"I *was* guilty. I had every intention of marrying his fiancée, heaven help me, until he and my father caught up with us."

He stared straight ahead.

"You took all the blame on your own head and lost your birthright for it," Mary Ann said thoughtfully. "For someone who pretends to be quite heartless, that was remarkably . . . gallant."

"Gallant! *That's* a pretty word for it," he scoffed. "Was I supposed to denounce her as the wicked seductress who toyed with me as a diversion from her aging bridegroom's ponderous attentions? *That* would have done wonders for my *amour propre.*"

He gave a long sigh.

"Honor is a peculiar concept in a man's world, Miss

Whittaker," he continued. "Losing one's head over a lady might be attributed to youthful high spirits and forgiven over time. But cowardice? Never."

"So, your father disinherited you in the face of the scandal, and you set out to embarrass him by setting up as a professional gamester."

"Why not?" Lionel said with a shrug of his shoulders. "I had been bred to administer my father's fortune and property, and now they would never be mine. In my stupidity, I actually made an attempt to secure a respectable post as an estate manager. Unfortunately, my wicked reputation had preceded me, and none of my prospective employers wanted a rake like me anywhere near his female relatives or servants. Meanwhile, for the first time in my life I could gamble every night if I chose to do so. In fact, I was *forced* to gamble every night because my father cut off my allowance. Before I knew it, the weeks turned into months and the months into years."

He shook his head in self-reproach.

"Now you know the whole sordid story."

"Oh, my poor darling," she said pityingly. "I don't know whether to kiss you or hit you for being so stubborn!"

"Well, I'd rather you kissed me," he said with a grin, knowing it was a mistake even as he drew her into his arms. She was too sweet, too soft, too warm—and her reputation was too vulnerable.

"I love you, Lionel," she whispered.

Lionel took her by her shoulders and held her at arm's length.

"You do not know what you are saying," he said as gently as possible.

"I do, and you know it," she replied. "We are not so unequal, you and I. Our fathers were both born gentlemen, regardless of how ill they behaved after that."

"My dear, are you by any chance proposing to me?"

he asked, trying to interject a note of levity into the conversation to dissuade her from her purpose.

"Yes. If they will not give us permission, let us run away together. *I* will not turn craven!"

"Absolutely not," he said firmly. "How can you even *suggest* such a thing to me?"

"Because I love you. I have been in love with you since I was fourteen years old. Lionel, I *prayed* that I would meet you again, because I was determined to marry you and no other."

Lionel sighed. He had suspected as much.

"My dear," he said kindly. "Look at me. I am thirty years old, almost as old as your brother-in-law. You would do much better to marry Julian, or even Renfield, if it came to that. They are closer to you in age, and either could provide well for you."

Mary Ann poked her finger into his chest.

"Julian! *Renfield!* Do you think I want to spend the rest of my life being bullied by your horrid stepmother? Or pandering to Lord Renfield's outrageous vanity? There is no love in that man's heart for anyone but himself. You would sentence me to *that?*"

"Mary Ann. Love," he said in that reasonable tone that made her itch to slap him, "look around you." He gave a wave of his hands toward the two pretty dresses hanging on the door of the elegant wardrobe, the gilt-edged cheval mirror, the sumptuous silk hangings and counterpane. "Do you think I could give you all this?"

"Silly man. You must know I would not expect it of you," she said reassuringly.

"Think, my love. You were poor once. You must remember what it was like."

"You are right, Lionel," she conceded. "I have been poor, and I remember very well what it was like. But because I was poor and survived it, I no longer fear it.

What I *do* fear is being buried alive in a marriage of the kind my mother would have for me."

She grabbed his lapels again.

"You *must* marry me, Lionel," she said softly. "You are the only man of my acquaintance who understands me in the least. Do *you* think I would make a docile and undemanding wife?"

"No, by God, I do not!" he declared as he kissed her hard enough to bruise her lips against her teeth.

"More," she breathed.

"No. Not now," he said, putting her away from him with a visible effort. "Not *here*. We must go back to the ballroom before you are missed, or—"

"There! You see!" shrieked Lady St. James as she propelled a white-faced Mrs. Whittaker into the room. Behind them was Sir Andrew St. James. "The blackguard is back to his old tricks. Now can you deny he is a villain?"

Good God. It was a nightmare.

A bloody nightmare.

"No," shouted Mary Ann, clinging to Lionel when her mother tried to pull her away from him.

"He forced his way into the bedchamber," Lady St. James said indignantly to Mrs. Whittaker, "and—"

"No! He did *not* force his way in here! I *brought* him here. So we could talk."

"Do not distress yourself, dear child," Lady St. James said to Mary Ann. Her eyes were hard as she glared at Lionel. "You are not the first innocent young lady to be taken in by his blandishments."

"No!" cried Mary Ann as Lionel's father took his arm and propelled him from the room. "This is all a terrible mistake!"

Lionel could have fought him—his father was hardly his match in strength—but what would have been the point?

"How dare you, sir!" his father demanded when they

were out of earshot. "How *dare* you disgrace me this way?"

"I have not been your son for ten years," Lionel said coolly. "Nothing I do has anything whatsoever to do with you."

"Barbara is in hysterics," Sir Andrew said with an accusing stare. "She won't let anyone approach her except her maid."

"Oh! I understand now," Lionel said sarcastically. "You and your wife just *assume* I am the one who attacked her." He gave a scornful laugh. "What appetites I must have! Forcing myself on two women in one night. Too bad Lord Byron left England before he could compose an ode to my prowess."

"It pleases you to make sport of it, does it?" Sir Andrew sputtered in indignation.

Lionel rolled his eyes.

"Father, can you honestly think I would hurt her or any woman? *Can* you?" Lionel said earnestly. "Please believe I would *never* do such a thing!"

When his father didn't answer, Lionel allowed his shoulders to hunch.

"You win, then," Lionel said, defeated. "I will leave. At once."

"It would be for the best," Sir Andrew said gravely. "My wife will make up some plausible story to explain her sister's injuries that need not involve you."

Was Lionel supposed to *thank* him for that?

Lionel gave a sardonic laugh.

"Good of her," he said bitterly. Once again Sir Andrew believed his wife's lies against Lionel's word.

His father frowned at him.

"I will have a servant summon Garland."

"No," Lionel said. "Garland is a good and loyal man, and he deserves a better master than I have been to him. Perhaps Lord Blakely can find a place for him in his household. Or perhaps you can find a place for him in yours."

Sir Andrew nodded.

"Very well," he said sadly. "Lionel, I—"

The proud old man fell silent and abruptly left the hall.

Lionel had his hastily packed satchel in hand and was about to lead Thunder out of the stable when a man's tall shadow filled the doorway.

"Here. Take it," Lord Blakely said abruptly as he tried to thrust the folded pile of notes into Lionel's hand. Lionel didn't need to count it to know how much it contained.

The bloody two thousand pounds. What a surprise.

With Lionel bribed with a sizable nest egg to hasten his departure, there would be no one to protest when Lady Cavenish's assault was laid at his door except Mary Ann. And she, poor deluded girl, could be dismissed as having fallen victim to his cold-blooded seduction.

Very neat.

"Keep it," Lionel snapped. "I don't need your damned money."

"I promised it to you, you've earned it and that's an end to it. I always honor my obligations," said Blakely. "Now take it, man."

"As a sop to your guilty conscience? Go to hell."

"As a sop to my . . . what *are* you talking about?"

He looked genuinely surprised, which made Lionel sneer in derision.

"Do you think I don't know your first inclination would be to break my jaw for being discovered in your sister-in-law's bedroom? Instead, you reward me with two thousand pounds to speed me on my way. Rather suspicious after some blackguard has beaten Lady Cavenish bloody."

"Beaten Lady Cavenish? Are you *mad?* She fell down

the stairs. Her sister said so. It was an unfortunate accident."

"Unfortunate accident, *hell!* Anyone who gets a good look at the lady's injuries will know *that* for a lie."

"Do you mean to tell me someone has physically attacked a guest under my roof?" Blakely looked furious. "But who would *dare*—?"

"And now *you* give me two thousand pounds instead of drawing my claret," Lionel goaded him. "Or do you save that tender treatment for defenseless women?"

"How dare you insinuate—!" Blakely appeared to be beside himself with anger. He broke off and clenched and unclenched his fists. "How could you think that *I*—?"

"I don't know." Lionel shook his head. "I wouldn't have thought it was quite in your style. But I wouldn't have thought the fair Barbara was, either."

Blakely gave an abrupt laugh.

"Hardly! At the risk of being ungallant, the lady makes me shudder. I don't think you would hit her, either, for what it's worth. And so I shall tell anyone who implies otherwise."

Amazingly, the viscount held out his hand and Lionel took it.

"Thank you for that, Blakely," he said quietly.

"As for the incident with Mary Ann, she came to me immediately and told me it was all her fault and not yours. I believed her, even when she insisted that you had behaved like a perfect gentleman throughout the whole embarrassing affair."

There was the slightest glimmer of a smile on Blakely's face, and Lionel suspected there was one on his as well. Mary Ann simply had that effect on people.

Then Blakely gave a regretful sigh.

"I am sorry it had to end like this, St. James."

"So am I," Lionel said. "Tell Mary Ann—" He broke off and shook his head. "Never mind."

"I suppose you also wanted to make sure I was leaving alone," Lionel added ruefully.

"I had no doubts on that score."

Lionel gave a snort of bitter laughter.

"I sometimes wonder how well you know her."

"Quite well, actually," Blakely said with one upraised eyebrow. "I know, for example, that she would accompany you to Scotland or to the stews of London, whichever you preferred, at one word from you. But I know *you* well enough to be confident that you would never give it. Thank you for that, St. James."

The viscount turned abruptly and strode back to the house, which was just as well, because Lionel was too astonished to say anything more.

Seventeen

"Line-all! Line-all!" cried Jamie as if his heart would break. Jemmy wept right along in sympathy.

It was enough to make the boys' nurse throw up her hands and join in the shrieking.

"They have been like this all morning," she told Vanessa and Alexander, who had come running for fear someone was murdering their darlings. It was the only explanation for such heartrending screams. "It's that nice Mr. St. James they want. He always gives them a ride on his horse's back of a morning when they go out for their walk."

"Line-all!" Jamie sobbed as Alexander picked up his elder son and balanced him on his hip.

"There now, son," Alexander said soothingly. "*I* can give you a ride on *my* horse."

"Line-all!" the child persisted with a mulish look on his face that reminded his affectionate mother strongly of her stubborn father-in-law, the earl.

"Well, we must find Mr. St. James at once, of course," Vanessa said calmly. Normally she was not one to inconvenience guests at a child's whim, but the boys were disturbing the Langtry children as well. The younger ones were standing in the doorway that led into the other nursery bedchamber with moist eyes and trembling lips despite Aggie and Amy's attempts to soothe them. Vanessa didn't miss the reproachful look in Aggie's eyes. It seemed that the heartless rogue Alexander had invited so reluctantly for Christmas had somehow become a favorite with all the children.

"He is gone, I'm afraid," Alexander said, picking up Jemmy with his free arm to see if *he* was interested in a trip to the stables with his father.

"Gone? Gone where?" asked Vanessa, surprised. "He left without saying farewell to me and the children? I never would have expected him to be so rag-mannered!"

"His departure was hardly his own idea," he said, with a meaningful inclination of his head at the nurse's curious face. "I will explain it to you later. After I take the boys outdoors to see if they will accept their poor father as a substitute for Lionel St. James."

Mary Ann regarded Lord Renfield dispassionately when he bowed and presented the perfect peach-colored rose to her as she sat alone at the breakfast table.

"For you," he said gallantly. "Only a perfect rose can hope to compete with your beauty."

"It *is* perfect, isn't it?" she said sweetly. "I forget the Latin name. It is very long. But the bloom is quite rare and it cost Alexander a small fortune to have the rosebush brought here for Vanessa's conservatory. They will be so glad you feel comfortable enough in their home to treat it as your own."

He didn't even pretend to misunderstand her.

"You don't like me much, do you, Miss Whittaker?" he asked with a big, confident smile on his face. Mary Ann knew very well that he continued his pretense of playing court to her merely for the sake of his abominable conceit and his love of a challenge. And, of course, the consideration that her brother-in-law's influence could be useful to him in his career.

"I neither like nor dislike you, Lord Renfield," she said indifferently.

"Which is what people often say when they dislike the person under discussion and do not wish to say so outright."

"Is that what people say?" she asked in a tone of false innocence.

His eyebrows rose.

"My dear Miss Whittaker, I must say I am surprised by your hostile tone. Whatever have I done to earn your displeasure?"

"Several things, not the least of which is your manner toward Mr. Lionel St. James."

"Is that all?" Renfield gave a negligent wave of his hand, as if to sweep aside such a trivial consideration. "The man is a mere gamester, Miss Whittaker. Naturally I was surprised to find myself rubbing elbows with him at a gentleman's residence. And concerned, of course, to see an innocent young lady such as yourself exposed to him."

"Regardless of your personal assessment of Mr. St. James's character, it behooves you to treat him with courtesy while you are under the same roof."

"Of course. Did I not say I was surprised to see him when we arrived? I'm afraid I said the first thing to Lord Stoneham that popped into my head."

"You will give me leave to tell you, sir, that I do not believe you have ever, in your whole life, uttered a single word without calculation."

"Miss Whittaker," he said in a mock injured tone. Even so, he looked as if he were enjoying himself. He thought they were *bantering,* for pity's sake! "You wrong me quite dreadfully."

Amazingly, he reached out and tilted her chin up so her lips would be close to his.

"If you do," she said with a false, sweet smile, "I shall scream the house down."

"Quite the spitfire, aren't you, my dear?" he said, laughing. But he did release her and back away.

"You were gone from the ballroom for quite half an hour at the beginning of the evening," she said with narrowed eyes. "Where were you?"

"Did you miss me, my sweet?" he asked lightly. But she could tell he was startled by her question. "If I had known that, I certainly would not have gone."

"Where were you?" she asked again. "Did you have an assignation with a lady, perhaps?"

"Ah, I begin to see why I am in your black books. You have no cause to be jealous."

He would have tried to kiss her again, but she pushed him away with both hands braced against his chest.

"You flatter yourself, sir," she said. He was the one who had been with Lady Cavenish. Not Alexander. She would stake her life on it.

"I see, Miss Whittaker, that I would be better served to present my attentions and my rose to a more receptive audience," he said archly.

"Quite," she said. "And I would do it soon, if I were you, before it goes quite brown around the edges."

To Mary Ann's indignation, he did just that. Not five minutes after he made her his bow and quit the room, she overheard him flirting with Melissa as she passed by another small salon.

"Only a perfect rose can hope to compete with your beauty," he said to the delighted young lady.

"Oh, Lord Renfield," Melissa gushed. "How lovely!"

Mary Ann rolled her eyes and walked on, determined to share her reservations about Lord Renfield with Melissa at her earliest opportunity.

But first, she had to locate Lionel without delay to tell

him about Lord Renfield's guilty reaction upon being questioned about his absence from the ballroom.

"Where is he?" Mary Ann demanded, hands on hips, as she stalked into her brother-in-law's office. "Garland said Mr. St. James is gone without a word to him."

Alexander looked up from his papers and sighed with foreboding at the sight of her flashing brown eyes and her lifted chin.

He didn't need to ask whom she meant. Not when he had just spent a fruitless hour trying to distract his sons from their heartrending pleas for him to go after Line-all and bring him back at once.

"I am warning you, Mary Ann, that I have heard all I wish to hear on the subject of Lionel St. James for one morning."

"Well, that is too bad," she said, sitting down in the chair in front of his desk as if she meant to stay. "You don't seriously think he attacked Lady Cavenish, do you?"

"No, but I can see why suspicion has fallen on his head," he said. "I am not at liberty to disclose the details, but he has reason to hold a grudge against the lady."

"You need not be so discreet. I know she is the one he is supposed to have abducted, but he is innocent. She inveigled the poor man into eloping with her ten years ago and then denied that she went with him willingly so she could marry the marquess."

"And you believed him." Alexander's look was almost pitying.

"Yes, I did. I also believe harming a lady is as alien to his nature as it is, for example, to *yours*," she said significantly. Her eyes were accusing.

"Mary Ann," he said, hurt. "You *cannot* believe *I* would

do such a thing! It is true that her attentions to me have proven to be embarrassing, but—"

"No. But neither do I think Lionel did it. If you are looking for a likely candidate as the villain, you might turn your eyes toward Lord Renfield."

"Renfield! Impossible! For the lord's sake, Mary Ann! He is one of the most brilliant young speakers in the House of Lords. And my friend."

"Nevertheless, he was missing from the ballroom for half an hour early last evening. I have never trusted the man."

"You just want to distract attention from St. James," Alexander said. "For what it's worth, I don't think he did it, either."

"And you showed him the door anyway."

"No, of course not. His father asked him to leave and he honored his wishes. Don't look at me like that! What could *I* do to stop him?"

"I'll wager you didn't try very hard."

"Blast it, Mary Ann! The man is not the sterling character you think he is. I wasn't going to tell you this, but I *paid* him to come to Leicestershire with us. It cost me two thousand pounds to get him to accept Vanessa's invitation to the house party. And, for your information, I paid him anyway, even though he had agreed to stay with us until the New Year."

"And then what?" she bit out.

"I don't believe I understand you," he said evasively. He couldn't quite look her in the eye.

"You made him promise never to see me again after that, did you not?"

"So, he *did* tell you," Alexander said in disgust. "I should have known he would go to you and paint me as the villain in this melodrama."

"No, he did not. But I know *you,* Alexander," she said, reaching out to cover his hand with her own. "No brother could be so protective of me. I should imagine Lionel is fortunate not to have found himself drugged and transported halfway to China by now."

"Indeed, he is," Alexander said ruefully. "Mary Ann, I would do *anything* to keep you from being hurt."

"How like you," she said with a sigh. "Alexander, I am a grown woman. I know what I want. And it is *not* any of the sterling characters you and Mama have been trying to bring up to scratch for the past two years."

"You want *him*, I suppose," Alexander said in disgust. "You are just like your sister Lydia."

"Precisely," she said with a smile. "And look how well *that* turned out."

"Oh, yes!" he said sardonically. "That turned out *wonderfully* well. She and her small child follow the good lieutenant and his cavalry regiment on various postings throughout the kingdom, living on his army pay, which, as a former officer, I can tell you amounts to virtually nothing."

"She didn't marry Edward for his money."

"It is a good thing!"

"She married him for love. The same reason I am going to marry Lionel."

"Has he had the infernal cheek to ask you? Has he?" Alexander demanded.

"Of course not. *I* asked *him*. So, where *is* he?"

"I wanted so much more for you."

"Tell me!"

She made a restless movement, as if she would fly from the room. Alexander knew she was entirely capable of mounting a horse to go careering over the countryside after her chosen man.

"Mary Ann, *listen* to me," he said desperately. She looked into his face. Good. He took her hand. "My dear, if he feels the same way about you, he *will* come back for you. Maybe not today. Maybe not tomorrow. But he will come to you in London, perhaps, after we return, and I will not forbid him the house. You must allow the man to retain *some* of his pride, and to go haring off after him as if he were your lost chick would be to unman him."

Mary Ann bit her lip.

"I will have to do something for him, I suppose," Alexander continued, giving the documents on his desk a dispirited little rustle. "I wonder if he has any aptitude as a secretary. Since Dunston left, my papers and correspondence have been in a shocking muddle."

"Thank you, Alexander," Mary Ann said, kissing him on the cheek. Her eyes were shining. "I knew you would see reason."

Reason. Alexander gave a snort of mirthless laughter. The girl was mad.

"Do not thank me yet," he said. "You have to convince your mother, and she has her heart set on your becoming Viscountess Renfield."

"I'd rather die," she snapped.

Happily for Mary Ann's continued existence, Lord Renfield had turned his attentions in quite another direction.

"Mary Ann, I could shake you," said her mother. "Lord Renfield had been paying his attentions to you again, but you were so cold to him that now he's making up to that Melissa St. James."

"Then perhaps you should address your complaints to *him,*" Mary Ann suggested.

"No, missy! I am addressing *you,* because you gave him not a single word of encouragement."

"And why should I? Mother, I *loathe* the man!"

"I know what it is—you have your eye on Mr. St. James." Her lips were pursed with disapproval. "Well, any man who would visit with a young lady in her bedchamber is no gentleman!"

"I invited him, Mama. To *talk!*"

Mrs. Whittaker threw up her hands.

"There are rooms all over this house in which you may *talk* with a young man!"

"But there was a ball in progress! There was nowhere to be private."

"Private is for when you are safely married, my girl! I am quite put out with Mr. St. James, and it is just as well he left the house. Who knows what might have happened if you had not been discovered—although I wish it had not been Lady St. James who discovered you. This is *most* embarrassing, but I hope she has enough discretion not to inform the whole household."

"Is that all you can think about? My reputation?"

"Yes!" The woman's usually mild eyes were fierce. "It's the only thing you have of value at your age."

That morning at breakfast, the guests were full of praise for the ball. Obviously none of them were aware that a lady had been assaulted in one of the salons or that Mary Ann had been found in a compromising situation with a man, for which she could only be thankful.

Still, it quite ruined her appetite to see the languishing glances Melissa and Lord Renfield cast at one another.

"He's going to ask me to marry him. I know he is!" Melissa whispered to Mary Ann after the ladies had withdrawn to the parlor and left the gentlemen to themselves. "That wretch Lionel! How *could* he have gone away, just when he is wanted to toast my happiness!"

Her accusing look told Mary Ann whom she blamed for Lionel's defection. Her horrid mother would naturally tell Melissa that her rogue of a half brother had been discovered alone with Mary Ann in her bedchamber.

"I am not any happier about it than you are," Mary Ann said glumly. "I wish he had not gone. He did so only to protect my reputation. And to please your father, of course."

"Then it is as I thought," Melissa said. "You *are* in love with him. We shall be *sisters!*"

Mary Ann gave a sigh of weariness.

"I hope you are right," she said, "but I am becoming discouraged."

"I am *determined* that you shall marry Lionel, if it is what you both want," Melissa said. Her eyes were alight with a new scheme. "You shall be one of my bridesmaids. And I shall invite Lionel, no matter *what* Mama says, so—"

Mary Ann laughed at the girl's optimistic plotting.

"Just like all married ladies—you will be eager to marry your friends off."

"How lovely it will be," Melissa said with a sigh.

And so it would, Mary Ann thought, if her friend's affections had fastened on *any* gentleman but Lord Renfield!

Barbara stared with dull eyes at her sister as if Lady St. James were a stranger. Indeed, she wondered if she *ever* had known her closest blood relative.

"The most glorious thing!" Beatrice crowed. "Lord Renfield is going to offer for Melissa. I just *know* it!"

"How could you even *consider* marrying your daughter to that man after what he has done to me?" Barbara cried out in horror.

She had recovered from her fainting spell burning with fever. Her eye was blackened, her nose was sore with bleeding and her arm was black and blue. At first her speech was barely intelligible.

Her sister had calmly refused Lady Blakely's offer to summon a doctor when she had inquired after her guest's health and learned that she was too unwell to come to breakfast. Barbara, Beatrice insisted, had fallen down the steps. The afflicted lady's tale of an attacker was merely a delusion brought about by her fever. Of course, there would be no question of removing her from the house when the holiday was over, she added, smiling.

Especially if Lord Renfield still occupied it. Melissa must have *every* chance of marrying a title.

"Silence!" Beatrice hissed, taking Barbara's wrist in a grip that hurt. "You will *not* ruin Melissa's chances of attaching Lord Renfield!"

Barbara's eyes widened. Her sister had thrust her into an unhappy marriage, but the marquess, at least, had never offered her violence.

"You cannot mean to give your daughter to him when you know what he did to me!" she said in disbelief.

"I know nothing of the kind," Beatrice said, looking Barbara straight in the eye. "You are merely confused."

"I am *not* confused!"

"Besides, Lord Renfield would never use Melissa so," Beatrice said complacently. "Melissa is a sweet, well-brought-up young lady who will do her duty both as a daughter and as a wife without complaint. She would never provoke him to violence, as you have done."

"So, what has happened to me is my own fault," Barbara said. Her lower lip wanted to quiver, but she refused to let it. Not in front of *her.*

"Of course. What else could he do when you *threw* yourself at him in that brazen manner? Of course he refused to elope with you. How could you have suggested such a thing?"

Barbara hung her head. She had been so desperate for comfort that she had blurted out the whole story to her loving sister. This was a big mistake. She should have *known* Beatrice would use her confession against her.

"I'll have you know, sister dear, that I had every reason to believe Lord Renfield's affection for me was real and permanent," Barbara declared.

"Was that before or *after* he blackened your eye?" Beatrice said sweetly.

"I can't let you do this thing," Barbara said.

Renfield had threatened to kill her, and Barbara would never forget the look of smug satisfaction on his face as he made his threat.

Barbara was afraid of him, yes. But she couldn't let her innocent niece marry him now that Barbara was aware of the violence that seethed beneath that hard, polished surface.

"I am going to tell Melissa the truth about him," Barbara said, steeling her resolve.

Beatrice's face turned purple with rage just before she dealt Barbara a ringing slap across the cheek. Barbara let out a shriek of outrage and burst into tears. It wasn't the pain that hurt her, it was the betrayal. At one time she believed that Beatrice, though misguided in her determination to marry her to the marquess, genuinely cared about her. Now she knew that Beatrice had never cared about her at all.

"You won't get the chance," Beatrice said with a sneer on her face that distorted it into an ugly mask. "I am afraid you are suffering from a delirium, dear sister, and you will have to be confined to this room for your own safety and protection."

"You can't do this to me," Barbara cried.

"I can, and I will," Beatrice said. Her lips were pursed, which showed all the fine lines that radiated from them.

With that, she stalked out the door, and Barbara heard the key turn in the lock.

"Give me the key, Beatrice," Sir Andrew said calmly as he joined his wife on the sofa in the parlor that afternoon.

"I beg your pardon, my dear?" she asked. "I do not understand you. Which key do you mean?"

Sir Andrew noted that her complexion did not vary in color nor her eyes shift with the lie. His wife was a deceiving, scheming, manipulative woman, but, God help him, he had loved her.

He had lost his son because of her machinations. He was not going to lose his daughter as well.

"The *key*, madam," he said coldly, holding out his hand.

"Andrew," she said with a pleading look in her eyes. "I did it to protect all of us."

"And what of my son, madam? Was that for *us* as well?"

"Andrew," she cried out as he crossed the room to the threshold, where Mary Ann Whittaker was waiting.

His wife's voice ended on a sob, but Sir Andrew didn't look back.

Eighteen

Lionel had gotten only as far as the village inn when he had to stop because of the falling snow and the dark roads.

Thanks to Lord Blakely's largess, he could actually afford a room. It was shabby. It was cold. The mattress was lumpy and smelly, and the sheets were highly suspect. But it was shelter. At least poor Garland would sleep in a warm bed tonight.

He found out the following day as he prepared to continue his journey on horseback to London, however, that Garland was less than grateful for his sacrifice in leaving his servant behind.

"*There* you are!" Garland shouted as he confronted him in his room. The old man snatched Lionel's shirt out of his hands and refolded it, clucking all the while like a disapproving hen. "I've a mind to *let* you wear mangled shirts after you disgraced me before the whole of Lord Blakely's household!"

Lionel's mouth fell open. He never had seen his mild-mannered valet in such a passion.

"*Disgraced* you! I was trying to spare you from making a dashed uncomfortable journey in the middle of the night," he said, hurt. "And where did you expect to ride? Perched behind me on the saddle like a swooning Medieval maiden?"

Garland rapidly continued refolding all of the shirts

Lionel had stuffed into his traveling case. He made it look a lot easier than Lionel now knew it was.

"Everyone in the house is looking for you," Garland grumbled in outrage, "and I, your own valet, had no idea where you'd gone."

"Who is looking for me?" Lionel asked.

Garland threw up his hands.

"Miss Whittaker. Your sister. Your brother. The nurse who takes care of Lord Blakely's twins. Miss Amy and Miss Aggie." Garland gave him a beady-eyed stare. "And I had to admit I had no idea where you were gone."

"How did you know I would be here, then?"

"The roads are a glare of ice. Lord Blakely's butler told me there is only one inn in the village. Where else could you have gone in the middle of the night?"

"I should have known you would come after me as if I were a truant child," Lionel said, shaking his head in wonder.

"Yes, you should. Come along, now, sir," Garland ordered, picking up the traveling case in a poor imitation of a deferential servant. "The carriage is waiting."

The carriage? Lionel shrugged and took this with a grain of salt. No doubt Garland had commandeered one of the farm carts.

"It doesn't matter if you've got the whole of the bloody House of Lords waiting. I'm not going back there."

"That's enough of *that* nonsense, young master," Garland said with a huff of annoyance as he led his way outside. He was not ready to forgive Lionel for leaving without him, obviously, and if Lionel wanted his shirts and shaving things, he had no choice but to chase Garland down.

"Give me that traveling case," Lionel demanded. Garland gave an injured snort and set a smart pace out the door of the inn. "I told you, I am *not* going back—"

Lionel broke off when he saw the black traveling carriage pulled up at the front door of the inn. It was not the homely gig he had expected.

He knew this coach well. It was showing a bit of wear about the edges, but as usual it was polished to a high gloss. Inside, it was large enough for a small boy to set out his toy soldiers and stage a major battle on one of the seats.

A footman opened the door and let down the steps.

"Father?" Lionel said in disbelief when the proud old man descended them.

"I have come to fetch you to Lord Blakely's estate," Sir Andrew said.

"Last night you ordered me to leave."

"Today I am here to *ask* you to return with me."

Lionel stared at his father for a long moment. Then he nodded and got into the coach.

Lord Renfield lighted one of Lord Blakely's excellent cigars and leaned back in the leather chair behind his host's desk. Blakely had asked Renfield to meet him here, no doubt to discuss some bit of pending legislation in the House about which Blakely wanted his opinion.

He had reason to be complacent. With Lord Blakely and the Earl of Stoneham as his mentors, he could go as high in government circles as he pleased. The office of prime minister was not out of his reach.

Renfield also congratulated himself that his courtship of Melissa St. James was a masterstroke. The girl was pretty, well-connected and well-dowered. More to the point, nothing could be more calculated to endear himself to Lord Blakely's sentimental household than a romance at Christmastide. He was of a mind to set up his nursery. It was time.

The Lady Cavenish debacle had blown over, as he knew it would. Mary Ann Whittaker might suspect something havey-cavey, but she could prove nothing. It was all he could do to keep a straight face when Lady Blakely told her properly sympathetic guests that Lady Cavenish was confined to her suite after having fallen down the stairs. Renfield knew the vain, silly cow wouldn't dare show her damaged face in company.

There had been no witnesses, after all, to his treatment of her. If it came to his word against hers, who would believe the word of a flighty marchioness of questionable family who was known for her extramarital intrigues over the word of an upstanding member of Parliament and the intimate of such powerful men as the Earl of Stoneham and Lord Blakely?

Renfield smiled in greeting when Lord Blakely strode into the room.

"Blakely! Excellent cigars, old man."

"I am so glad you approve," his host said. His smile didn't come anywhere near his eyes.

Renfield sat up straighter. This was not the friendly comrade he often dined with in London.

"Is something wrong?" he asked.

"Several things," Blakely said stiffly. "Come in, gentlemen."

To Renfield's astonishment, Lionel St. James entered the room flanked by his grim-faced father and brother. Both of the younger men looked at Renfield as if they cheerfully would have drawn his claret.

"Melissa, my dear," Renfield said when that lady entered the room and sat beside her father. Her face was white, and there was ice in her eyes when she looked at Renfield. Was it only a few hours ago that she had smiled at him as if he personally had strung the stars in the sky for her pleasure? Renfield extended his hand to her, but Sir Andrew St. James lashed out and rapped him smartly across the knuckles with a newspaper.

"Keep your hands off my daughter, sir," he rasped.

Lady St. James came into the room and stood by her husband. Her face was blotched with tears, and her nose was red.

"You may sit over there," Sir Andrew said coldly to her. He pointed to a chair by the door.

"This is all a mistake," Lady St. James said tearfully as she patted her daughter's hand.

Melissa gave her mother a glacial stare. Almost meekly, Lady St. James obeyed her husband and took the chair by the door.

"Lord Renfield," Blakely said, calling the meeting—for that was what this seemed to be—to order. "I think it would be best if you leave my house."

"I say," Renfield replied with a nervous laugh. "Is this some sort of joke?"

"No joke," Blakely said. "I know what happened last night between you and Lady Cavenish. I will not have a guest assaulted under my roof."

"The woman is demented," he said in a creditable assumption of surprised amusement. "Good God, Blakely! You know what she is."

Lionel gave a smothered exclamation and started to rise, but his father caught his arm and shook his head at him. Even so, the look Lionel gave Renfield quite made the blood drain from his face.

"Come in, Lady Cavenish," Blakely said kindly.

Her face was pale, her eye was still bruised, but she was composed and dignified as she faced her attacker.

"I did not fall down the stairs as my sister said," she said clearly. "It is you, Lord Renfield, who did this to me."

"Melissa," Renfield said, turning to that young lady. He assumed she was the weakest link in the chain, and the one most likely to be swayed by the heartrending look of appeal he gave her. "You cannot believe this. There is no proof."

"My aunt has named you. That is proof enough."

Renfield opened and closed his mouth.

"You are making a mistake," he said desperately to Blakely.

This was a disaster. If news of his assault of a noblewoman got out, he would be ruined!

"I think not," Blakely said. "You may go now. I have already instructed your man to pack your clothes."

"Why don't you ask *him* where he was that night?" he said, pointing at Lionel. "Everyone knows he and the lady have a past."

"My son," said Sir Andrew, drawing himself up to his full height, "would never harm a woman. *Any* woman."

"He's a gambler. You disowned him yourself."

"A mistake I am about to rectify," the old man said. "Lionel, I owed it to Julian to discuss this with him first, and he has agreed. You are to be reinstated as my heir. And with that, I beg your pardon for misjudging you all those years ago. Barbara has confirmed that you were innocent of having abducted her."

"Barbara?" Lionel said, looking at her in wonder. "You have done this for me?"

"As I should have ten years ago," she said wryly. "I hope you can forgive me someday for being such a coward."

"But I—of course I forgive you."

"I am content, then," she said, walking to the doorway where her maid waited to escort her back to her room. "Thank you for . . . last night."

Speechless, he carefully kissed her on the cheek and watched her with pity in his eyes as she left the room.

Lady St. James gave a long, shuddering sigh and directed a look of reproach toward her husband.

"Andrew," she whispered. "How *could* you do this to Julian?"

Before he could answer, Mary Ann Whittaker strode into the room with fire in her magnificent eyes.

"What are you doing here?" she cried out as she looked around the room at the grim-faced observers. She didn't miss the tears on Melissa's face or the look of shock on Lionel's.

She took a bulldog's stance in front of Lionel as if she would defend him from his detractors. "I will not hear a word against him, do you hear me?"

Lionel took her hand and kissed it.

"Peace, my dear," he said softly. "It seems I am to be made respectable again."

Renfield gave a snort of disgust and stalked from the room. Lord Blakely shook Lionel's hand and followed, presumably to make sure the villain actually left the house.

Julian gave Lionel a rueful smile and shook his hand. He kissed Mary Ann on the forehead.

"Be happy, my children," he said with a droll smile.

Julian offered his arm to his sister. "Come along, Melissa. You did well." With a slight hesitation, he crossed the room and offered his other arm to his mother. She gave a watery sniff and accepted.

Sir Andrew looked at his wife's bowed head and back at Lionel.

"She wanted to be a good stepmother, you know," he said. "And a good sister. And a good mother."

"And a good wife, I suspect. We will sort it all out later, Father, when we are at home," Lionel said kindly.

"Yes. Home," his father said, smiling. "It will be good to have you at home, Son."

"Thank you, Father," Lionel said, shaking hands with him again.

"Men!" Mary Ann said in disgust when Sir Andrew had left the room. "Ten years of estrangement, and when it is over you *shake hands*."

Lionel grinned.

"And what would you have us do? Fall weeping into one another's arms? Kiss the air above one another's cheeks like society maidens? I should like to see his face if I attempted any such thing."

"Well, shaking hands seems a bit *too* manly and dignified," she said. "Do men never show affection to one another?"

"No, darling," he said, smiling as he bent to kiss her. "We save all that for you."

They broke off when pandemonium erupted outside the door. It sounded as if a herd of elephants were clattering by.

"What is it?" Mary Ann cried out. She had one hand pressed to her heart.

A plump, bedraggled young matron wearing a green traveling costume of approximately three seasons past and her hat wildly askew over her light brown curls appeared in the doorway.

"Lydia!" Mary Ann cried out. "Lydia! Oh, how we have missed you! We thought you would be in Scotland until spring at least!"

She flew into the lady's arms and succeeded in tipping the dowdy hat from its precarious balance.

"It's Lydia! My sister," she said to Lionel.

"So I gather," he replied, smiling.

Lydia's eyes narrowed at him.

"And you are?" she asked, transforming immediately into a protective elder sister.

He held his ground under that shrewd scrutiny.

"Lionel St. James, madam, at your service," he said with a bow.

"Lydia, Mr. St. James is the one who pawned my ring and gave us the Christmas goose," Mary Ann said hurriedly. "Seven years ago. You *do* remember?"

"Indeed?" Lydia said, approaching Lionel and peering

up at him. "So *you* are our Christmas angel, Mr. St. James." She slipped one arm in his and offered the other to Mary Ann. She looked from one smiling face to another.

"Come along, my dears," she said. "I can see we have much catching up to do."

Nineteen

It was Christmas Eve, and the children's excitement was at fever pitch.

Jamie and Jemmy were bundled to their eyes in soft blankets and waved to Mary Ann as their father carried them out to a small sleigh that had a fat pony between its shafts.

According to tradition, only the men of the household went out into the woods to haul in the Yule log, but the twins weren't about to be left out of an excursion into the night by torchlight.

Mary Ann and her sisters waited just inside the door in their hastily donned coats to wave them off. Lady Madelyn, getting into the spirit of the thing, fluttered an exquisite, lace-edged handkerchief as her husband passed by. He caught her hand and kissed it.

"You'll be good," he said with mock sternness to his younger niece as she huddled against Lady Madelyn's skirts.

"I'm always good," said the child with the mischievous eyes.

Her uncle gave a good-natured snort and ruffled the little girl's pretty blond curls. The child's elder sister, Melanie, waited with her brothers beside the sleigh. Unlike the other females present, she wore sturdy boots, a warm hat, a muffler around her mouth and nose and gloves that would probably be ruined before the night was over.

No slave to fashion—yet—Melanie insisted on helping with the Yule log, too. Why should the men and boys have all the fun?

Aggie and Amy agreed, although *their* idea of fun was sampling the plum cake Vanessa's cook had prepared for the feast.

Grinning and jostling one another like boys, Julian and Lionel came out of the house next.

Lionel slowed and smiled self-consciously when he saw Mary Ann looking at him. She gave him a cheery wave.

In her prejudiced eyes, he was the most handsome man in this company of handsome men.

Mary Ann recalled how, when she first saw Lionel, she could imagine him in armor fighting dragons. Or in flowing shirt and leather scabbard fastened at his lean hips defending a ship from pirates. She was his lady, seeing him off to battle, praying that he would return to ask her hand in marriage.

Joyful chaos had reigned in the household when Lydia, her husband, Edward, and her one-year-old son, Quentin, arrived. Mary Ann had no chance for a word alone with Lionel after that.

Lionel had always claimed Mary Ann was too good for him; now, with the reinstatement of his birthright, would his father decree that he was too good for *her?*

"Come along now, Lionel," Julian said, taking his brother's arm. "There will be time enough to flirt with Miss Whittaker when the work is done."

To Mary Ann's surprise, Lady Madelyn burst into sentimental tears.

"Lady Madelyn?" Vanessa said in concern. "Are you ill?"

"No, my dear," she said, dabbing at her eyes. "I am

just thinking of last year, when everything between Robert and me seemed so hopeless. And then Christmas came."

"The season of miracles," Mary Ann said.

"Precisely," said Lady Madelyn, dimpling, as she gave Mary Langtry, her niece by marriage, an affectionate hug. "I cannot see the torches any longer. Let us go inside before we catch our deaths."

"Goose!" cried young Mary when she saw the splendid bird on the table. "I *love* roasted goose!"

Unlike the other meals in the house, Christmas Eve dinner was laid out on the table all at once, and family and guests would serve themselves. Along with the goose, mountains of steaming potatoes, slabs of plain bread and butter, and bowls of unpeeled oranges and walnuts adorned the table, along with the plum cake.

This was a reminder of that long-ago Christmas season when the Whittaker ladies had no servants to wait upon them, and no dinner for them to serve.

And no hope, until a kind stranger came to their aid.

On Christmas Day, Vanessa's kitchen staff would provide an extravagant array of lavish Continental dishes for the feast. But Christmas Eve was a night for the Whittaker ladies to commemorate their Christmas miracle.

"It wouldn't be Christmas Eve in this house without a fat goose on the table," Lydia said with a glance at Mary Ann. "How exciting that the provider of the feast will share it with us this year. Tell *all,* dearest! *Where* did you find him? And when is the wedding?"

"Lydia, darling," said their mother repressively. Delighted as Mrs. Whittaker was to have Lydia and her family join them for Christmas, she had always deplored her second daughter's tendency to blurt out exactly what was on her mind. "Do try for *some* discretion."

"Nonsense. Did you see the way the man *looked* at her?" Lydia made a show of fanning herself. "An offer is forthcoming. Believe me."

Mary Ann wished she could be as sure.

"Lydia, I'm *so* glad you came," she said tearfully.

"Well, I can see nothing in that for you to get all maudlin about, love," Lydia said bracingly.

"They're coming! They're coming!" cried Mary, who had been watching for the approaching torches at the window while the ladies drank tea and gossiped. Everyone clattered to the front hall to cheer when the men came into the hall.

The log was enormous, and Lionel was in the lead with it. Mary Ann could see his muscles bulge under his coat. He caught her looking at him and smiled. He looked different, and Mary Ann realized that the haunted, guarded look was gone from his eyes. His face was open and boyish. His smile was full of affection when his father blustered in to supervise the placement of the log.

Of course, Mary Ann thought. His mind would be full of the family he had thought he lost. At dinner, he sat between his father and Melissa who, thankfully, seemed inclined to regard her aborted courtship by the odious Lord Renfield as a lucky escape rather than a tragedy.

Lionel had reconciled with his father. It was what she had wanted, wasn't it?

She was covered with shame when she recalled how she had begged him to run off to Scotland with her. Now he could have almost any woman he wanted in the whole of Britain.

Would he want *her*?

"A toast!" Alexander called out from the head of the table. "To Lionel St. James, the donor of the first Whittaker goose and the author of this charming tradition."

"Here, here!" echoed the other men as they raised their glasses of the local ale that was part of the tradition, as well.

How the *ton* would have stared to see the Earl of Stoneham, his high stickler of a sister, Lady Letitia, and Lady

Madelyn peeling oranges for small children with fingers greasy from the goose.

Mary Ann felt a moment of perfect happiness as she glanced around the table at all the people she loved best in the world.

Whatever else happened, her dreams had come true.

Her family was healthy and happy and well fed. She *did* find Lionel. And Lionel was reconciled with his family.

And Lydia, her beloved elder sister, had made it home for Christmas after all.

For now, it was enough.

The goose of Christmas Eve, 1819, was only a delicious memory, and still Lionel had not approached her.

It was perfectly natural, Mary Ann told herself, for him to be so caught up in his family that he had no thought to spare for her.

She was an outsider, after all, and Lionel had much to learn before he could assume his father's honors.

To her disappointment, Lionel wouldn't be staying to welcome the New Year.

Sir Andrew was eager to get his heir home and introduce him to the land steward, his bankers and all the others who would acquaint him with his renewed status. Then, at Lady Cavenish's request, Lionel and Melissa would accompany her to collect her children from the marquess's primary seat. They would travel on to Italy, where Lady Cavenish intended to make her peace with the man to whom she had been married for so long. Perhaps the marquess wasn't the man she loved, but he was her husband and the father of her children.

If he was willing to forgive her for her transgressions, she would forgive him for his. Perhaps they could begin again with honesty between them.

And, if nothing else came of the trip to Italy, Melissa would enjoy a taste of Continental society to compensate her for the loss of the odious Lord Renfield.

Before they embarked upon their sea journey and a possible reconciliation between the marquess and his marchioness, the St. Jameses would celebrate the New Year in their own home as a family for the first time in ten years.

Mary Ann was trying very hard not to be selfish, but she wanted Lionel to be with *her.*

Maybe when his affairs were settled, he would come back and ask her to marry him.

But then it wouldn't be Christmas anymore.

As if her thoughts had conjured him, the object of her most cherished hopes appeared in the doorway. His cravat was still askew from a lively pre-bedtime tussle with the twins.

"Mary Ann! I have been looking all over for you. Where have you been?" he asked.

Actually, she had been in her room, crying for a little while. Then she had changed into her favorite warm, long-sleeved, russet-colored woolen gown and let her hair down to cascade down her back in the hope that she would look suitably romantic and approachable if Lionel chose to seek her out, but *he* didn't need to know that.

"Where have *you* been?" she countered. To her horror, her voice sounded cross and petulant. This was *not* the way she wanted to begin what she hoped would be a tender scene.

She bit her lip in consternation.

"Here," he said softly. "Let me do that."

She gasped with relieved laughter when he bent and nibbled her lower lip.

"Delicious," he added between exquisite little kisses. He ended by touching his lips to her forehead and setting her slightly away from him. "But I get ahead of myself."

He took her hand and drew her toward the hearth, where they sat before the blazing fire.

"Mary Ann, will you marry me?"

She gasped.

She had hoped. She had prayed. And the moment had finally come!

"Yes!" she said, throwing her arms around him. "I accept."

"Good. That's it, then."

He stood and started to leave the room.

She snagged him by the elbow and yanked him back down beside her.

He was teasing her, of course.

Something new between them.

"What took you so long?" she demanded, giving him a smart rap on the shoulder.

"Your brother-in-law," he said, catching her hand and playing with her fingers.

"Alexander? Because he had objections?" she asked indignantly.

"No, my sweet. Because it was difficult to find him alone. First, I had to make my intentions known to my father. Then I had to extricate his lordship from his sons, who made an eloquent plea for another trip to the woods by torchlight, on Thunder this time. And my brother, who lost no time in putting himself forward to Blakely as a candidate for the vacant post as his secretary now that he's a second son and is no longer expected to have grand political ambitions. I practically had to haul Julian out of Blakely's office by the scruff of his neck to get the great man alone! Then, after I made my formal petition for your hand—which he accepted with flattering haste, I am happy to say—*my* father must needs join the meeting to point out my sterling character and glowing prospects to Lord Blakely."

He broke off with a laugh at the look of astonishment on Mary Ann's face.

"Yes, you may well stare!" he said. "Then Julian barged back in to offer me his congratulations, and we had to drink to the match—and all this before I could find you to ask you to marry me."

He gave a long sigh.

"Being respectable is *such* a silly business, love. Maybe we should run off to Scotland after all."

"All right, if you wish," she said loyally, willing to abandon her visions of bridesmaids dressed in pink tulle and a cake the size of a house, if it would please him.

"Not on your life!" he said, laughing. "We are going to do the thing properly."

He took her hand and kissed it.

"I wish I had a ring to put on your finger, my love," he said ruefully.

"You've already given me one."

She pulled the golden chain out from the neckline of her gown to show him the tiny pearl ring.

"To think this once fit on your finger," he mused, turning it over in his hand. "Is *this* what you have been hiding at the end of that tantalizing golden chain?"

"For seven years," she said, kissing him on the cheek. "I *knew* you'd come back to me."

At that moment, the clock chimed midnight.

"Happy Christmas, my love," he said softly. "I am the happiest creature on earth."

"Not quite. At least not for long," she said, taking him by the hand. "Come. Let us wake up Mother and tell her I am a betrothed woman."

Epilogue

Lionel and Mary Ann spent the first day of the New Year together after all, for they decided they couldn't wait until spring for a fashionable wedding at St. Paul's in London to become husband and wife.

Why, indeed, should they wait for spring, they reasoned, when there was a veritable flower garden available at Lord Blakely's estate?

As dawn sent the first rosy streaks across the sky on New Year's Day, Mary Ann was escorted to the conservatory by her bridesmaids.

Only one of them wore the pink tulle Mary Ann had envisioned; fortunately, Amy had not yet outgrown the pink dress she wore at Easter.

And if the cake wasn't *quite* as big as a house, it wasn't through lack of a valiant effort on the part of Vanessa's pastry cook. Vanessa, Lydia, Aggie and Melissa wore their favorite pastel dresses for the occasion, which meant Mary Ann's bridesmaids represented almost every color of the rainbow.

It had taken the eager bridegroom exactly two days to ride to London on horseback for a special license and a wedding ring, and Vanessa rather less than that to arrange Mary Ann's bridal bouquet from the most fragrant pink roses and white orchids in her conservatory.

Mary Ann wore her ivory beaded gown with Vanessa's lace wedding veil. To everyone's surprise, Lady St. James insisted on lending the bride a diamond comb to secure the veil to the back of her head.

"If I am dreaming, don't ever wake me up," Lionel whispered when Alexander handed her into his safe-keeping.

He was so handsome that he took her breath away.

"My prince charming," she said with a sigh.

Julian, who as his brother's best man was standing close enough to hear these expressions of revolting sentimentality, rolled his eyes and gave a snort of laughter.

"My poor, deluded girl," Lionel said in affectionate self-deprecation.

Just then, as the pastor intoned the opening words of the wedding service, a strong shaft of light from the rising sun turned the glass walls of the conservatory into a bright, glowing prism of color.

The wedding guests, composed of all the first families in the neighborhood, gave a collective sigh of pleasure.

"It's a miracle," Aggie blurted out in excitement as her mother impaled her with The Look.

"A miracle, indeed," whispered Lionel as he favored his bride with a broad, audacious wink.

Julian gave a smirk of good-natured scorn. Mary Ann didn't doubt that her bookish future brother-in-law could discourse at length on the scientific explanation for such a phenomenon.

Men! What did *they* know of miracles?

Mary Ann smiled up into the beautiful sea-green eyes of the man she adored and knew that the true miracle was having all the people they loved best in the world gathered here to share their happiness.

Could she have dreamed of a wedding day more perfect?

Perhaps Mary Ann could not, but her mother certainly could.

"It was a pretty wedding," Mrs. Whittaker conceded later as she dabbed her eyes with a white lace-trimmed handkerchief, "but I so wish I could have prevailed upon Mary Ann to wait until spring. Such a hasty marriage is sure to create an *off* appearance."

Lady Madelyn raised one shapely, russet-colored eyebrow.

"Oh, I think not, ma'am," she said gently. "Not when it becomes known that *I* was among the wedding guests. Am I not right, Lady Letitia?"

"Certainly, my dear," that haughty lady said with a gracious nod. "We will know how to depress the pretension of anyone who dares utter a word of criticism."

Mrs. Whittaker smiled. If Lady Madelyn and Lady Letitia meant to take the couple up, there was nothing more to be said. Mary Ann and Lionel's position in Society was assured.

Not that either of them cared a rap for all that.

Mrs. Whittaker and Lady St. James exchanged a look of maternal long-suffering when Lionel suddenly swept his bride up into his arms and made her shriek with laughter.

"He was always so boisterous," Lady St. James said with a sigh.

"And my girls were always so headstrong," Mrs. Whittaker said with an answering sigh, adding hastily, "all except for my Amy, that is. You will not find a more sweet-tempered, pretty-behaved, obedient girl in all of England."

She lowered her voice conspiratorially and leaned closer to Lady St. James, drawing her attention to Amy, who was smiling adoringly into Julian's laughing eyes.

Amy always had looked excessively pretty in pink.

"She will be fifteen in April, which would make her

the perfect age in a year or two for a steady young man of . . . did you not say your Julian is just turned two-and-twenty?"

ABOUT THE AUTHOR

Kate Huntington lives with her family in Illinois. She is the author of five Zebra Regency romances and is currently working on her sixth, which will be published in July 2002. Kate loves hearing from her readers, and you may write to her c/o Zebra Books. Please include a self-addressed, stamped envelope if you wish a reply.

More Zebra Regency Romances

Embrace the Romances of
Shannon Drake

The Queen of
Romance

Cassie Edwards